NEVER TRUST A COWBOY

BY
KATHLEEN EAGLE

MILLS & BOON

Published in Great Britain 2015
by Mills & Boon, an imprint of Harlequin (UK) Limited,
Eton House, 18-24 Paradise Road, Richmond, Surrey, TW9 1SR

© 2015 Kathleen Eagle

ISBN: 978-0-263-25107-4

23-0115

Harlequin (UK) Limited's policy is to use papers that are natural, renewable and recyclable products and made from wood grown in sustainable forests. The logging and manufacturing processes conform to the legal environmental regulations of the country of origin.

Printed and bound in Spain
by CPI, Barcelona

Kathleen Eagle is a *New York Times* bestselling author, teacher, mother of three grown children and grandmother of three children. Many years ago she fell madly in love with a Lakota cowboy, who's taught her about ranching and rodeo, Sun Dance and star gazing, and family "the Indian way," making her Grandma to more beautiful children than she can count. Visit her at www.kathleeneagle.com and "friend" her on Facebook.

In loving memory of Phyllis Eagle McKee

Chapter One

Delano Fox enjoyed watching a smooth heist in progress the way any skilled player might be entertained by another's performance. Sadly, under the starlit South Dakota sky on the flat plain below his vantage point the only real skill on display belonged to a blue heeler, and even he was a little slow. Del was going to have to forget everything he knew about rustling cattle if he was going to fit in with this bunch. Otherwise he'd find himself itching to take over, which wasn't the best way to get in thick with thieves. Even rank amateurs had their pride.

One by one, six head of black baldy steers stumbled into a stock trailer, each one springing away

from the business end of a cattle prod or kicking out
at the biting end of the dog. There was no ramp, but
a jolt of fear helped the first two clear the trailer's
threshold. When the third one tried to make a break
for it, Ol' Shep lunged, crowding the animal against
the trailer door. The guy manning the door cussed
out both critters, while the one handling the prod
added injury to insult by missing the steer and con-
necting with the dog. It would've been funny if he'd
stung the other man with a volt or two, but Del in-
stantly set his jaw at the sound of the yelping dog.
Inexperience was curable, but carelessness could
be a fatal flaw, and lack of consideration for man's
best friend was just plain intolerable. The best cow-
hand of the lot—the one with paws—jumped into
the bed of the jumbo pickup, where he shared space
with the gooseneck hitch.

Two shadowy figures climbed into the growling
workhorse of a pickup that was hitched to the stock
trailer, while the third—the prod handler—hopped
into a smaller vehicle—a showy short box with an
emblem on the door—parked on the shoulder of the
two-lane country road. He would be Del's mark.
One of them anyway. He would be local, and he
would be connected. Rustlers were high-tech these
days, and they used every resource, did their research, found their inside man.

Del didn't go in much for high tech. He did his
research on the down low, and he had already had

a private, persuasive conversation with a man he knew to be one of the two hauling the stolen stock. The job he himself was looking for would soon be his.

He chuckled when he passed the sign welcoming him to the town of Short Straw, South Dakota, promising, You'll Be Glad You Drew It.

Maybe, but there was bound to be somebody in the area who wouldn't be. Del knew how to handle the short straw. He'd drawn it many times.

He followed the sawed-off pickup at a distance, which he kept as he watched the driver pull up in front of a windowless storefront emblazoned in green neon with what would have been Bucky's Place if the *P* were lit up. The *B* flickered, trying mightily to hang on to its dignity, but it was *ucky* that cast a steady glow above the hat of Del's mark, the man who had just helped steal six head of cattle. Del could see enough of the guy's face now to add a few pieces to those he'd already collected. He could now read the Flynn Ranch emblem on the pickup door. So far, so good. The driver wasn't much more than a kid, early twenties, maybe. The steers might well belong to his father. Wouldn't be the first time the heir decided to help himself to his inheritance a little early. Del just hoped Junior had the power to hire and fire ranch hands.

It took Del all of thirty seconds to disable a tail-light on Junior's pickup.

A typical edge-of-town watering hole, Bucky's was shades of brown inside and out. Customers were lean and green or grizzled and gray, but they were all on the same page at Bucky's. They were winding down. Two guys sat side by side at one end of the bar, a third sat alone at the other, a man and a woman exchanged stares across the table in a booth and pool balls clicked against each other under the only bright light at the far end of the establishment.

"I'm looking for the owner of the Chevy short box parked outside." Del was looking at the bartender, but he was talking to anyone who'd noticed his entrance. Which would be everyone.

"That'd be me." The kid who'd wielded the cattle prod waved a finger in the air and then turned, beer bottle in hand. He wore a new straw cowboy hat and sported a pale, skimpy mustache. "What's up?"

"The name's Delano Fox." Del offered a handshake. "If you're with the Flynn ranch, I was told you might be hiring."

Junior admitted nothing, but he accepted the handshake. "Who told you that?"

"Ran into a guy who said he'd just quit. Told me to look for a red short box with a taillight out. Your taillight's out."

Junior frowned. "You been following me?"

"More like following up on a tip. Not too much traffic around here. Hard to miss a single taillight."

"When did he say he'd quit?"

"Maybe he said he was *about to* quit. I don't remember exactly how he put it, but if you're not short one hand, you soon will be. You hire me, you won't need anybody else. I'd get rid of the other guys."

The bartender chuckled.

"Only got one hand. *Had*, sounds like. Where did you run into him?"

"Couldn't say. Somewhere along the road." Del tucked his thumbs into the front pockets of his jeans and gave an easy smile. The way to play the game was to keep the questions coming and the answers on the spare side. "After a while they all look alike. Faces and places and roads in between."

Junior nodded toward the empty stool beside him.

"Did he mention his name?" Junior asked as Del swung his leg over the stool. "Or mine?"

"Flynn was all he gave me. Said he was helping move a few steers and that the guy driving the red pickup might be hiring. That last part was all that interested me."

"Brad Benson. Tell me why I should hire you."

So this wasn't Junior. One missed guess, but it was a small one. As long as the kid could hire a new hand, he would be hiring Del.

"I'll put in a full day every day." Del sealed the deal with a sly smile. "Or a full night. Whatever you need."

Benson took a pull on his beer, took his time setting it down and finally glanced sideways at Del. "How about both?"

"A guy's gotta sleep sometime. But yeah, calving time, I'm there. Workin' on a night move once in a while? I can do that, too."

Benson didn't bite. "Where have you worked before?"

"Just finished a four-month job on a place west of Denver. The Ten High. Foreman's name is Harlan Walsh." Walsh was his standard reference. Harlan knew the drill. Del had actually worked at the Ten High, just not recently.

"If Thompson don't show up tomorrow—"

"Pretty sure he won't." *Damn sure he won't.* Thompson had been most cooperative once Del had ruled out all other options.

"If he don't, then we'll try you out. The Flynn place is sixteen miles outside of town on County... Well, I guess you already know the road. We pay thirty a day to start, six days a week. You'll have the bunkhouse to yourself, and you'll get board with the family." The grin was boyish. "Bored, too. Get it?"

"Either way, as long you've got a good cook in the family."

"You can always get yourself a microwave," Benson said, tipping the beer bottle in Del's direction. "Oh, yeah, and you answer to me. It's my stepdad's operation, but he's getting on, and we're trying to get him to take it easy."

"Understood."

"And if it turns out you're more skilled than most, more…specialized…" Benson's lips drew down in the shape of his mustache. "You could bump up your income, put it that way."

"Like all good cowboys, I'm a jack-of-all-trades." Del tapped his knuckles on the bar as he dismounted from the stool. "With resourcefulness to spare."

"Just to show your appreciation, spare some on buying the second round."

Del chuckled. There hadn't been a first round. "My employer always gets the better end of the deal. I'd suggest the other way around if I wasn't dog tired. I've been on the road awhile."

"And I'd show you to your room, but I ain't ready to hit the road."

"I'll be there by eight."

"Breakfast's at six."

Del glanced at the shot the bartender set down next to Benson's beer, and then gave his new boss a slight smile. "I'll be there by eight."

The Flynn Ranch sign hung high above the graveled approach five miles south of the scene of the previous night's crime. Del's first thought was how easy it would be to alter the Double F brand that adorned the intersection of the gateposts and the crossbar on both sides of the entrance. A seasoned rustler would have it done by now even if he was hungover. Del was betting Benson was fairly new to the game and that last night's haul still carried the Double F. He doubted Benson had any authority to recruit new thieves. A man new to the game only stole his own cattle for show, to convince family, friends and FBI that he was among the victims. And by peeling off some skin and dropping it into the game, he bought himself some street cred. But he'd have to keep up appearances on both sides. Del looked forward to seeing whether Benson was any more serious about his acting than his rustling.

The red Chevy pickup was parked kitty-whompus beside an old two-story farmhouse that probably had been a local showplace in its day. The right front tire had crushed a bed of pretty blue-and-white flowers. Some of the once-white paint on the house was peeling, and some had been scraped. The covered porch looked as though it had recently been painted.

Del mounted the steps to the sprawling porch and rapped on the screen door. He heard movement, peered through the screen and saw a pair of chunky rubber flip-flops—neon green, if he wasn't mistaken—sitting on a rag rug in the dim alcove.

The bare feet that belonged to the shoes appeared at the top of the stairs beyond the alcove, paused and then ran down like water bouncing over rocks. Del was fascinated by the quickness of the flow and the lightness of the feet. He'd never seen prettier. He watched them slip into the rubber thongs, pink toenails vying for his attention with bright green straps. The colors spoke volumes about the woman who came to the door.

He wasn't sure why he wanted to hold off on looking up. The colors were cheerful, the feet were pretty and their owner probably belonged to his new boss. But for some reason he wanted to take her in bit by stirring bit.

She wore jeans that ended partway between her knees and her curvaceous ankles—Del admired a well-turned ankle—with a sleeveless white top over a willowy body. Her neck was pale and slender, chin held high, lips lush and moist, dark hair pulled back, and her big blue eyes stared at him as if he were some kind of a rare bird. Maybe he was looking at her the same way. He couldn't tell.

"Mornin'." Del recovered his game face and touched the front edge of his hat brim. "I'm looking for Brad Benson."

He watched her shut down any interest he'd sparked. "You came to the wrong door."

"If you wouldn't mind pointing me to the right one…" He smiled. "Sorry. Del Fox. I'm your new hired man."

"I don't have an *old* hired man. Or a man of any kind behind any of my doors. And if I did, it wouldn't be Brad Benson."

"My mistake. I saw his pickup out here." He was pretty sure she hadn't meant to be funny, but he had to work at keeping a straight face. His new boss was clearly in trouble. He stepped back and nodded toward the side of the house. "Looks like his pickup anyway."

She pushed the screen door open and ventured across the threshold, took a look and planted her hands on her hips. "It does, doesn't it?"

"Same plates and everything. Must be around somewhere. You wanna tell him I'm here?"

"I want to tell him to get his pickup out of my flower bed. Or maybe you'd tell him for me when you find him."

"Should I try the doghouse?"

"I don't have one. My dog..." She stepped past him and surveyed the yard. Her tone shifted, the wind dropping from its sails. "Should be chewing on the seat of your jeans right about now."

"Guess he ain't hungry. Maybe he got a piece of Benson."

She gave her head a quick shake, banishing some momentary doubt that had nothing to do with him or with Benson. "Maybe you should check the pickup." She nodded toward the dirt road. "It's another mile and a half to the new house, and you can be sure Brad didn't walk. How drunk was he when he hired you?"

"Couldn't say."

"And you wouldn't if you could." She lifted a

lightly tanned shoulder. "It really means nothing to me, but it might make a difference to you."

"I'll check the pickup." He touched two fingers to his hat brim and stepped back. "Sorry to bother you. Sign says Flynn Ranch, and Benson wasn't clear on where the house would be."

"I'm Lila Flynn," she said quickly. "Brad is my stepbrother. He lives down the road with his mother and my father."

"In the *new* house." He smiled, grabbing the chance to start over. "You get the home place."

"And you'll get the bunkhouse out back if Brad remembers hiring you." Suddenly retreating, she cast a backward glance. "Like I said, check the pickup."

Before the screen door slapped shut, Del caught the edge of a smile, the flash of blue eyes. Slim chance, he thought, but the door to making a second first impression had been left ajar.

Driveway gravel rattled under Del's boot heels as he approached the red short box pickup. Benson's chin rode his collarbone as his head lolled from one side to the other.

"Good morning."

Benson opened his eyes halfway, squeezed the right one shut again and squinted the left one against the sunlight until Del's shadow fell across his face.

"Remember me?"

"Yeah, I remember." Brad waved a fly away from

his face as he slid his spine up the back of the pickup seat. "You said you had all the experience I might be looking for. You haven't seen Thompson around, have you? The guy you're replacing?"

"Not since last night. Your sister's the only person I've run into since I got here."

"*Step*sister. She sure can be a bitch, that one." Brad draped one hand over the steering wheel and rubbed his eyes with the other, muttering, "The kind you wanna bring to heel."

"She said I could have the bunkhouse out back."

Brad dragged his hand down over his face. "She did, huh?"

"She did, but it's up to you. Like you said, you're the boss."

"You just said the magic words. What's the name again?"

"Del Fox. Do I need a key?" No answer. "You got anything you want me to do before I stow my gear?"

"What time is it? You probably missed breakfast."

"I had breakfast."

"That's right. You got yourself hired and called it a night. Showed up on time, too. Maybe we'll keep you around." He fired up the pickup. "Make yourself at home. Fox? It's Fox, right? Sorry, I'll be more hospitable after I've had some coffee." He pointed to the cabin fifty yards or so behind the house, not far from an old red barn with a lofty arch roof. "That'll be your home sweet home. We've got another barn down at the new house, but that's the only bunkhouse. Who needs two bunkhouses these days, right? Or two hired hands."

"One of each is more than most places have." And having a cozy log cabin to himself was a vast improvement over his usual accommodations.

"Everybody around here is downsizing. Either that or diversifying."

Del glanced to one side and noticed a fenced area close behind the house with a swing set, a little play-house, a sandbox and more kid stuff. For some rea-son he was surprised, and he turned quickly back to Brad. "Which is it for you?"

"You'll have to ask Frank. My stepdad. Can't seem to make up his mind." Brad shifted into gear. "Take your time. I'll be getting a slow start today. If Thompson shows up, tell him to come find me."

Del dropped his duffel bag just inside the bunk-house door and drew a deep breath. Pine pitch and dust. Pine was fine, but dust— He grinned—busting dust was a must. He opened the window between the two single beds and heard someone whistling— warbling, more like—and then calling out for Bingo. From the window he had a view of distant table-top buttes and black whiteface cows grazing on buffalo grass. A meadowlark sang out, and a cho-rus of grasshoppers responded. He liked the sights and sounds, most of the smells, and he decided he wouldn't be living out of a suitcase for a while. He liked the idea of hanging up his shirts and putting his toothbrush on a shelf.

He was wrestling with the drawers in a broken-down dresser when the warbler tapped on the door.

"It's open."

The woman with the big blue eyes, Lila, peered inside. "It's always open, but you can have a lock on it if you want."

"I don't use locks. You knock, I'll answer." *Gladly.* No man in his right mind would lock her out. She was a pretty woman trying to pass for plain, and it wasn't happening. The world owed women like her a clue. She'd get noticed no matter what. "You need any help?"

She pushed open the door with the edge of a straw laundry basket. "I brought you some bedding. I have a feeling you won't see Brad before supper-time, and I don't know what's here."

"Somebody's clothes. If anyone comes looking, they're in that box on the bench outside the door." He nodded toward the floor in front of the dresser, where he'd tossed the sheets he'd stripped off the beds. "I wasn't sure what I was gonna do with those."

"I'll take care of them." She peeked into the bathroom. Her hair was clipped up on the back of her head in a jaunty ponytail. "I guess I could spare

you some towels. Doesn't look like the last guy..."
She turned and handed him the neatly folded bedding. It smelled like early morning. "I still can't
find my dog," she said quietly as he set the laundry on the bed.

"I didn't see anything on the highway."

"You weren't really looking."

"You want me to? I've got nothing else to do. As
far as I'm concerned, I've been on the payroll for
about an hour now."

"He's pretty old. Doesn't usually go far from the
house."

"You probably don't want your kids to find him
first. How old are they?"

"My kids?" She gave him a funny look, as if
maybe he'd been reading her mail. And then the
light went on. "Oh, the play yard. I do some day
care. *Other* people's kids."

"Maybe other people's kids took your dog."

"The kids aren't here on the weekend. Bingo. Little black terrier. If you see him..." She wagged her
finger and chirped, "Bingo is his name-o."

"Ain't much of a singer, but I'm a hell of a whistler." He reproduced her warble perfectly. "Like
that?"

"He won't be able to tell us apart." She smiled.
"I'm not a hell of a whistler."

He smiled back. "You're a singer. You can have

my whistle for a song. I'll drive out to the highway and walk the ditches. How's that?"

"As you said, you're on the payroll, but you don't work for me." She started for the open door, did an about-face on the threshold and came back. "But it's a generous offer, and I'll take you up on it. In return I'll—" she grabbed the laundry basket by one handle and lifted her shoulder "—owe you one."

"Two." He presented as many fingers. "If one good turn deserves another, I'll take two towels. If you're sure you can spare them."

"I'll even throw in a washcloth."

He came back empty-handed and genuinely relieved. He liked dogs and didn't want to see her lose hers. He was good at turning on the charm for people no matter what he was feeling, but there was no pretense when it came to dogs. He'd lived with them, worked with them, learned to respect them without exception. Lila Flynn was a dog person. He could be himself with her on that score.

Plus, she'd brought him clean sheets without him even asking.

He parked his pickup near the bunkhouse, taking care not to block the view from the door or either of the windows. He had to smile when he noticed the broom and mop leaning against the bench on the little plank porch, along with a bottle of Pine-Sol. His favorite.

His return didn't distract her from pinning laundry to the clothesline in her backyard. He watched her from his new front yard, a little below the level of hers. Another nice view. The summer breeze batted blue denim and white cotton around and toyed with Lila's hair. He enjoyed watching. But if she was still feeling friendly toward him, he would enjoy shooting the breeze with her even more.

Especially if she'd found her dog.

"Any luck?" he asked when he reached the clothesline. She shook her head. "I didn't find anything on the highway." She paused for a moment. "Guess that *is* lucky, when you think about it." He ducked under an assortment of socks and turned so he could see her face. "Maybe he's off huntin' rabbits."

She didn't look at him, but she smiled a little.

Try again, he told himself. "I haven't been around too many terriers. Maybe not big enough to take down a rabbit."

"Size doesn't matter. Not to a terrier. They'll take on all comers." She snapped a wet shirt straight. "So to speak."

He was pretty sure she meant to be funny, but her face wasn't showing it.

He smiled big. "A little confidence buys a lot of respect. From most comers anyway."

"Thanks for your help." She slid her empty basket across the grass and touch tested a sheet. "Oh, right. Towels." She headed for another line. "Let me fold these sheets and then I'll see if they're dry."

He stepped forward to help, and they fell naturally into the two-person task of taking down sheets and folding them, meeting corner to corner, brushing hand to hand.

"So your dad's kicking back and letting Brad take over?" Del asked.

"Take over what?"

"The cattle operation. Sounds like your brother's stepping up."

"*Step*brother."

"Stepping on toes, is he?" He surrendered a smooth sheet to her charge. "Kinda feelin' my way here. You hire on with a family operation, you like to get a feel for the pecking order before you step into the coop. Don't wanna slip on anything the first day."

She bent to the laundry basket. "You'll be on the bottom."

"And you?"

"I'm not part of the order. There's no pecking in my coop."

"Good to know." He unpinned a stiff towel. "Is the bunkhouse part of the peck-free zone?"

"That's up to you. Do you have any terrier blood in you?"

He laughed. "I can sure tell you do."

"Here you go." She selected a pair of blue towels, started to turn them over but paused for a quick nuzzling. "Mmm. Don't you just love the smell of air-dried laundry?"

"Mine usually comes from the Laundromat."

She straightened suddenly, her attention drawn to something just outside the play yard. "Bingo!" She dropped the towels in the basket, ducked under the clothesline and took off toward a mass of conspicuous greenery. "Bingo?"

A telltale hiss prompted Del to follow her. The woman could sure move.

"Lila, back off," he shouted, and she froze at the edge of the vegetable garden. "Step back real slow. That's not Bingo."

The critter sprang a good two feet above an orderly row of bush beans. It was a badger.

"He's got something cornered," Del said quietly.

"Bingo!"

He grabbed her from behind, pulled her to his chest and clamped his arms around her. "Good Lord, woman."

He held her close and still, and they watched the badger disappear and a rattlesnake spring forth. Snake down, badger up, like squeezing a long balloon, alternating ends. It might have looked funny if desperation hadn't been alternating with brutality.

"Damn. We're not even on their radar."

"I've never seen anything like it," Lila whispered, mesmerized by the hopping and hissing.

"Good thing Bingo isn't around. He'd be right in the thick of it."

"You were close." And he wasn't letting her go.

They were close. She turned her head and looked up at him, and for a moment he was as deep into her as the snake was into the badger. Just as surprised. Just as engaged. Her eyes were crystalline, as blue as the sky, and damn if they weren't almost as big. They had power.

It wasn't until she turned back to the combatants that he was able to draw breath. He loosened his arms reluctantly but didn't let go, and she seemed a little reluctant to be let loose. An even match, neither could gain without yielding. It was too late to compromise, too soon to take prisoners.

Too late for a handshake; too soon for a kiss.

"I can't tell who's winning," she whispered.

He chuckled. All things considered, he'd made gains.

"No, really," she insisted. "Can you?"

"I think they're both hurtin'. Probably both wishing they'd never met."

Finally the two animals jumped apart as though someone had blown a whistle, then turned tail and took off in opposite directions.

"What do you s'pose that was all about?"

"Home." His arms were a little lazy about letting her go. "Some dank hole in the ground. Had to be. They sure as hell weren't fighting over the same female."

"As long as it wasn't about my dog."

"I didn't hear either one call out, 'Bingo!'"

"You're funny." Her little smile settled the urge to apologize. "I like that."

"You really love your dog. *I* like *that*." He grinned. "How about going to supper with me?"

"You're expected at the other house."

"That's what I mean. How about going with me?" He shoved his thumbs into his front pockets. "When I get my first paycheck I'll take you to the best café in Short Straw."

"I thought you'd been to Short Straw."

"I've been to Bucky's Place. Had a sausage-and-egg sandwich there this morning. Fresh out of the microwave."

"I can make you some lunch."

"My stomach's still working on that sandwich. Iron gut chippin' on a rock."

"It doesn't get much better in Short Straw. As for Flynn ranch fare…" She glanced past him, nodded toward the road to the other house. "Here comes your boss. Do you have much experience working cattle?"

"I'm a good hand, yeah."

"Don't let Brad get to you. He likes to give orders."

The red Chevy short box turned off the road

and sped across the grass in their direction. Brad leaned out the window. "Hey, Fox, you ready to get to work?"

"Been ready."

"Hop in and I'll show you around." He pulled on the brim of his straw hat. "What's up, Lila?"

"Have you seen Bingo?"

"What, that old dog? You lost him?"

"I can't find him."

"Then he must be dead somewhere. I guarantee you, nobody would steal him." Brad caught Del's eye, expecting an ally. "Good for nothing, that dog. Except making a lot of noise."

"Only when you come around," Lila said.

"Recognition of the alpha. One thing about dogs, they know their place." He stroked his scraggly mustache with thumb and forefinger, then grinned, basking in the perfection of his observations. "I'll keep my eyes peeled. If I see hide or hair, you want me to bag it up for you?"

"If you find him, I'd like to have him back. Del's already searched the right-of-way."

"*Del*, huh? Just remember he works for *me*, Lila." He watched Del slide into the passenger seat. "Don't let her boss you around, man. She likes to give orders."

"Just something to do while I was waiting on the boss."

Del's smiling eyes connected with Lila's as he propped his elbow on the open window and gave her a conspiratorial wink.

Chapter Two

Lila wasn't taking the new hand seriously. She'd known he was kidding when he asked her to go down to her father's house with him for supper. She had managed not to look out her kitchen window more than once or twice, checking for signs of life at the bunkhouse. She told herself she was only parking her horse in Dad's corral now because it was time to check in. She hadn't seen her father in more than a week, and she was suddenly missing him.

She stuck her socks in her boots and left them in the elaborate mudroom June had added to the plans for the new house, padded through a kitchen filled with the smell of beef and fresh bread—interesting, since she'd never known June to bake bread—past the kitchen table normally used for meals and ventured into the dining room.

"Well, look who's here," Brad said. "There's an empty chair next to me and one beside our new hired hand. Take your pick."

"Your new hired hand asked me to go to supper with him." Del almost managed to get out of his seat and pull out the chair before she claimed it herself. Lila tamped down a smile. "So I choose him."

"You should've told me you had a date, Del. We could've picked her up." Brad peered across the table at Lila. "How'd you get here? Don't tell me you finally decided to put the crazy woman in the closet and get behind the wheel of a car again."

She eyed him right back. "The horse I rode in on is helping himself to your hay."

Frank laughed. "My daughter is no crazier than I am, son. I'm taking up bread making. Watched one of them videos and got the recipe off the internet. How'd I do?"

"I knew he'd find it relaxing," June said. Her red hair looked freshly styled, the color skillfully revived. Dar's Downhome Dos had done it again. "It's very good, my darling. And you notice, the baker in the video was a man. The best chefs are men. So it doesn't surprise me that this bread is delicious. No more store-bought for us." She flashed Frank a doting smile. "No surprise, he especially enjoyed kneading the dough."

"What else has he been kneading?" Brad pulled a fake double take. "Never mind. We probably don't want to go there with our parents. Right, Lila? I mean, we're eating."

Once begun, half done, Lila reminded herself.

"He experimented with the dough hooks that came with that new mixer I got him, but that didn't do it for him. Right, Frank? I'd say mission accomplished, technique perfected. What do you think, Del?"

Del brandished the buttered heel he'd just torn into. "Great bread."

"There's more in the kitchen," Frank said.

"Just for you," June told Del. "When Brad said he'd hired a new hand, Frank was all about welcoming you with a good meal."

Frank gestured with the point of his table knife. "If you're as good as Brad claims, I'd like to keep you around for a while. Guess Thompson took off without saying too much. I never thought much of him, tell you the truth. Brad says he called a guy you worked for, what? Couple of years, right? Said you're a top hand." He turned to Brad. "Where'd you say that was? Colorado somewhere?"

"Denver," Brad said.

"So you came along at the right time. You mind puttin' up hay?"

"It was a four-month job," Del said quietly. "This last time. But I've worked for Walsh before. And I guess I wouldn't be much of a ranch hand if I minded putting up hay."

"I used to hate that part of the business, but nowadays, with the new equipment we've got, I can just—"

Brad's knife clattered to his plate. "I'll make sure Del has plenty to do, Dad. I drove him around all afternoon, so he knows what he's in for. He's like you. Says his cowboy ass ain't sittin' on no ATV. Right, Del?"

"Brad fixed me up with a good mount." Del glanced at Lila, an I'm-on-your-side look in his eyes. "Nice big buckskin."

"Hombre," Brad told Frank. "Figured you wouldn't mind."

"Best horse on the place." Frank grinned. "He should be ridden, and by somebody who knows how."

Between her father's grin and the look in the hired hand's eyes, Lila suddenly took heart.

"Sounds like something I've heard before," Brad said.

"That's what Rhett Butler said to Scarlett," June put in.

"Kissed." Lila attended to buttering her bread. Attention with a secret smile. "He said she should be *kissed* often."

"I don't get to many movies," Del said. "This Butler, is he a cowboy? You got a horse needs ridin' or a woman needs kissin', you find yourself a real cowboy. Ain't many of us left."

"Probably just as well," Lila said. "Hollywood isn't making many Westerns these days."

"*R-e-a-l,*" Del instructed. "Not *r-e-e-l.* The world is full of actors."

Lila flashed him a richly deserved smile.

"You like that?" His answering smile lit a true twinkle in his nearly black eyes.

"I do."

"What's going on here?" Brad said. "If I didn't know better…"

"You'd think I was rackin' up points with the boss's daughter. But I can already tell she doesn't give out easy points. I'm just trying to keep up with the conversation." Del glanced around the table. "Lila and I witnessed a rare sight this morning." He nodded at her. "You tell it."

"We watched a fight between a badger and a rattlesnake. They tore up my garden."

"I thought *I* tore up your garden," Brad said.

"You ran over a flower bed." She took Del's cue and kept going. "It was amazing. They really kept at it for, I don't know, five minutes, maybe… They just kept at it." She turned to Del. "Didn't they?"

A loaded look accompanied Del's nod. "Time stood still."

"In fact…" *Damn*, he was good-looking. Nearly black hair, chiseled cheekbones, angular jaw and no white-above-the-eyebrows farmer tan on this cowboy's face. Unless she was mistaken, he'd be head-to-toe brown. Lakota, probably. It took her a moment to turn her attention to her father. "Del caught me before I walked right into the fray."

"How awful. I hate snakes of any kind." June gave a tight end-of-story smile. "And I really hope you'll start joining us for supper regularly, Lila."

"I didn't have any kids today. Del helped me look for Bingo. I've been searching on horseback, still haven't found him." She lifted one shoulder. "So I was…in the neighborhood."

"I haven't seen the pup at all lately." Frank turned to his wife. "Have you? You've been out quite a bit getting groceries and whatnot."

"I thought he always stayed around your yard," June said, turning to Lila.

Lila nodded. "That's why—"

"Bingo is the first dog we've had around here since Lila left for college," June explained, apparently for Del's information. "I'm not a dog person. Kind of allergic." She turned to Lila. "I think that's why you decided to move into the old place when you came back, isn't it?"

"That's my house," Lila said.

"I know, but it's as old as the pyramids, all dark

and depressing. We'd like to see more of you. That's all I'm saying."

"I'm not far away, June. You have to drive past my house to get to the highway. We see each other all the time." Lila welcomed the mental distance that slid over her like a cool cloud. "And your hired hands are always perfectly positioned to keep an eye on me."

"That happens to be where the bunkhouse is," Brad said. "The men don't give you any trouble, do they? You tell me if they do. I never hire anybody without checking him out. And I don't tell them to keep an eye on you." He turned to Del. "I never told you to spy on her, did I?"

Del shook his head. "This was a fine meal." He tucked his napkin under the edge of his plate and slid his chair back from the table. "It's been a long time since I had any homemade bread. Sure was good."

"Now, listen, you tell her I never said anything about—"

Del chuckled. "In my line of work you quickly learn when to hold 'em and when to fold 'em. Hold your tongue, fold your napkin and leave the table." Which he did, all but the tongue-holding part. His calm, cool parting shot was aimed at Brad. "I can handle most any chore, but spyin' ain't one of 'em." He nodded at June. "Thank you, ma'am."

* * *

Lila found Del in the barn currying the buckskin. He'd had time to saddle up after making that break for it, killing the time she'd allowed to pass before she left the house. Nothing further had been said on the subject after he left. Maybe they all felt ridiculous. *Keep an eye on her.* If Brad had asked—and she had her doubts about that—Del would have refused. She'd only been around him for a few hours, but she'd learned a lot, and she had no doubt he would have said no.

"So that was awkward, huh?" She ducked under one of the cross ties and scratched Hombre's throatlatch. "I'm sorry."

"Forget it. Whatever that was about, it's for you guys to deal with."

"But we put you in an uncomfortable spot, and I'm—"

"Don't apologize. It had nothing to do with me." He glanced at her. "Unless you think otherwise?"

"I don't. I know you wouldn't go along with anything like that." She smiled. "I realize we just met, but I'm a pretty good judge of character. Brad can't push you into doing anything you don't want to. I'm surprised you're still here."

"I'm here to work, and I've been at this kind of work long enough to know when to excuse myself from the table." He ran his hand down the horse's back and patted his rump. "I'm the one who owes an apology. I asked you to come with me for supper, and then I didn't show up."

"You were working."

"I don't know what I was thinking. Should've taken my own pickup instead of getting in with Brad. But now that I've got this guy…" He lifted a familiar black saddle onto the buckskin's back. "Brad didn't tell me he was Frank's. You think he minds?"

"I think he's glad to have you ride him."

"Is he a good judge of character, too?"

"Sometimes. He's already taken a shine to you."

"So…" He gave the saddle cinch a firm tug. "Would you like some company on the ride back to your ancient digs?"

She smiled. "Would you like a tour of the ruins when we get there?"

"You got any mummies?"

"I had one, but she died when I was twelve. Now I just have a stepmummy." She gave a shy smile. She knew she was being too cute by half. She was far afield of her comfort zone. "You?"

"Mine's dead, too. So's my dad. Been a while, so, uh…" He lowered the stirrup. "We should cover new ground on the way back. I didn't get much chance to look close, flying around the pasture in Brad's pickup—hey, that man sure has a lead foot—but I tried to be on the lookout. You know, for…any kind of sign."

"See what I mean? You're obviously a nice man."

"You want me to throw a saddle on that pretty black?"

"I pull out my own chair and saddle my own horse." She smiled. "But thanks for the thought."

"Yes, ma'am." He touched his hat brim. "Always thinking."

The sun hovered above the sawtooth horizon and the air was still, leaving the horses to stir the grass and offering the crickets a quiet setting for their serenade. Lila had covered the side of the road before supper, so they took the south side, zigzagging separately, cutting across a wide swath. She knew the odds of finding anything weren't great, but every search was a chance, and she wouldn't rest until she knew for sure. She'd adopted Bingo from a shelter in Rapid City, and he'd seen her through some lonely times.

"Was he sick or anything?"

Lila looked up and saw Del staring at something on the ground. His dismount was as fluid as any she'd ever seen. Reins in hand, he squatted on his heels, picked something up and sniffed it.

"C'mon, Jackpot." She trotted her horse in his direction. "Anything?"

"Too old." He stood up and tossed his discovery. "A piece of something hairy, but all dried up."

"Why do I have a feeling you haven't always been a cowboy?"

"I don't know." He used the horn as a fulcrum and swung back into the saddle without benefit of a stirrup. Grinning like the boy who'd taken a run and jumped all the way over the creek, he adjusted his hat. "Maybe I started out as a trick rider."

She narrowed her eyes, considering, and shook her head. "What else you got?"

"I like to work my way up, one surprise at a time. Keeps 'em guessing." He braced his forearm over the horn and took a turn studying her. "Where'd you go to college?"

"Minneapolis." He'd started moving. She nudged her gelding to catch up. "Were you ever a cop?"

He gave her an incredulous look, caught himself and laughed. "How did you come up with that?"

"The way you examined the evidence."

"Too many detective movies and not enough Westerns, college girl. What did you study?"

"Art history, music, British history, literature—"

He whistled appreciatively.

"—business, library science."

"That's a lot of studying."

"I didn't quite finish," she said quietly.

A meadowlark answered Del's whistle.

"I'm listening," he prompted after a moment had passed.

"I had a bad car accident."

He let the words have their due. The grass swished, crickets buzzed, the sun settled on the sharp point of a hill.

"Hurt bad?"

"I wasn't. The person I hit… She was." She cleared her throat. "I don't drive anymore."

"Not at all?"

"Not at all."

More grass sound filled in.

"She okay now?"

"Were you ever a reporter?" she retorted stiffly.

He said nothing. He'd gone one step too far. Game over.

"Put it this way," she amended. "You don't strike me as the kind of man who usually asks a lot of questions."

"I'm not the kind who'd strike you at all. I'm the kind who'd do his job, tip his hat when you walk past him and keep his thoughts to himself."

"Sounds like we're two of a kind. Or *were*, until you took an interest in helping me find my dog."

"You'd do the same, right? It's all about the dog."

"We were talking about ancient history before," she reminded him. "Mummies and all like that. Been a while, you said. For me, too. And the passage of time helps. I know it does. It takes the edge off regrets, shuts down the what-ifs." They were riding slowly now, the search all but set aside. "She recov-

ered, but it took a long time, and it changed her life.
Don't ask me how it happened. It doesn't matter."

He nodded.

She knew she didn't have to tell him not to discuss it with anyone. It wouldn't kill her if he did, but somehow she knew he wouldn't. They had things in common, spoken and unspoken things. What things they were didn't matter as much as how they felt about them. They could move on without exchanging details.

"I have to find Bingo, no matter what. I have to bring him home."

"Do you have a picture of him?"

"You'll know him when you see him. He's the only little black terrier around. This isn't exactly terrier country."

"What's the cell phone reception like around here?"

"Terrible. You have to go up on a hill, and even then it's hit or miss. You're welcome to use my old reliable landline anytime."

"I was thinking if I find the dog and he won't come to me…"

"He loves cheese." She tucked her hand in her back pocket, pulled out a chunk of it wrapped in brown paper and reached between horses to hand it to him. "He won't care if it's a little squashed."

"Funny dog."

She smiled. "You two will hit it off just fine."

* * *

At breakfast the next morning Del was assigned his first official chore. No surprise, he was to ride the fence and check for breaks.

"Neighbor called and told Dad there's been cattle disappearing again. I'm gonna head down to the south pasture and start counting."

"If I find anything, you want me to fix it right away?" Since he knew where to look, he was going to help himself to a second cup of coffee. He gestured with the pot, and Frank offered up his cup for a refill.

"Well, *yeah*," Brad said. "That's one job you can be sure gets delegated."

"Just wanted to make sure."

"If we're missing cows and we don't find them, we'll let the sheriff in on all the details."

Frank took no notice. Either he didn't hear, didn't want to hear or his agreement went without saying. In any case, nobody was too concerned about preserving a possible crime scene.

Del took his time riding the fence along the dirt road that separated two Flynn Ranch pastures. He knew he would find the wire down less than a mile off the blacktop, but along the way there was a chance he might run across Lila's dog. He found himself hoping otherwise. This far from the house, it was bound to be a sad discovery.

A faint set of tire tracks in the dry ground led to

the hole in the fence. Three loose strands of barbed wire curled away from the steel post in three different directions. A qualified lawman would be able to get a clue or two, and fixing the fence wouldn't make too much difference. But it would make some. Not to Del, of course. He'd been a witness. Now he had to figure out where Frank fit in, and he knew better than to ask questions he didn't know the answers to.

He fixed the wire, and then he followed the fence line until it took a right turn at the highway. There he saw the grass stir. It could've been a snake or a grouse, but it wasn't. He knew before he reached the spot that he'd found the little black dog.

Not quite what he'd expected, but it was small and male and black. Who else could it be? And he was alive, which was a whole lot better news than he'd expected. Del whistled. The paper crinkled as he unveiled the chunk of cheddar.

"Got some cheese for you, Bingo. Come and get it, boy." He sank to his knees, and the pup bounded through the grass and pounced on the cheese. Del's left knee cracked in protest as he stood with his arms full of wiggly, scrawny, finger-licking dog. "I thought you'd be fuzzier. How'd you get this far from home on such short legs, huh?" The dog seemed a little young, but maybe that was because he was scared and hungry. He rooted around Del's shirt, struggled to get his nose in Del's scratching hand. "That's all I've got, boy, sorry. We'll go get you some more. Lila sure is gonna be happy to see you."

But she wasn't.

She petted the pup's head, but she wouldn't take him in her arms. "He's cute enough, but he's not my dog."

"What do you mean, he's not your dog?" Del put the dog on the ground, let him check out the furniture legs on Lila's front porch. "I found him not three miles from here, nobody else around. He fits your description. He's— You're pullin' my leg, right?" The dog sniffed Lila's bare toes. "He likes you."

Then he abandoned bare toes for black boot.

"Hee-yah!" Del ordered, and the dog looked up and cocked his head as though he needed a translation. And, of course, he did. Forgetting himself— more like forgetting his cover—Del had spoken in Lakota, his father's first language. "No. Don't you dare."

The dog wagged and whined.

Lila laughed. "He likes you even more."

"Only because I fed him. Hell, he loves cheese, just like you said." He jerked his thumb toward the porch steps and told the dog, "Show her you know where to pee."

Lila folded her arms imperiously. "He's not Bingo. He's too young, and he's not even a terrier."

"He's a little black dog. Bingo?" The wagging speed doubled. Del had to reward such obvious name recognition by picking him up again. "Yeah, Bingo. She's messin' with me, ain't she?"

"He'd wag his tail for you if you called him Stupid. He's not my dog."

"Damn." Del lifted the dog's muzzle and looked him in the eye. "You sure?"

"I've never seen him before. I'll ask my kids' parents when they drop them off, but my guess is, you've found yourself a dog."

"What do you mean, *myself*? I've been looking all over hell for *your* dog."

"He doesn't have a collar. Either somebody dropped him off or..." Lila scratched the furry head. "Are you lost? Did you run away? Speak."

"Ruff!"

"Aw." Del put the pup down and offered a hand. "Shake." Paw plopped into hand. Del flashed Lila a grin. "And you can just tell he's housebroken, too."

"Lucky for you," she said. "Because I'm not looking for *a* dog. I'm looking for *my* dog. Unless somebody comes looking for him, the finders-keepers rule applies."

"I like dogs, but there's no way."

"Yes, there is. I see the will in your eyes." She glanced at the dog. "And thirst in his." She retrieved a pan of water from the other end of the porch and set it down. They watched him go for it. "Bingo..."

When he comes back, Bingo will let him stay with you, but not with me. So you'll have to take care of him, and you might as well start now."

"No, I can't…" Del slid the pup a sympathetic glance. "Somebody's been teaching this dog tricks. That somebody's looking for him as we speak."

"And if that somebody comes to call, you're in luck. Or out of it, which would be—" Lila levered an eyebrow and growled "—*ruff.*"

"I'm bettin' somewhere there's a kid crying over this dog." The eyebrow arched again, and he groaned. "You got some food for him?"

"I have all kinds of stuff you'll need for him. I'll drop it off in the bunkhouse. And I have kids coming this afternoon. I promise I'll ask about him."

"They'll love him." And they'd all play with him, give him a name.

"If nobody comes looking for him, you'll have to get him vaccinated before he can be around my day care kids." She patted his arm. "I'm holding out for Bingo."

"I looked all over, Lila. This little guy needs—"

"All over? You've only been here a couple of days. This place is a lot of all over." She watched the pup for a moment, stepped back and shook her head. "It was an honest mistake. I don't want to keep you from your job."

"You're not. I was on my way to find Brad." The little black dog was right behind Del when he left.

He turned, looked down at the wagging tail, the expectancy in a pair of big brown eyes, and he chuckled. "Yeah, you can come along."

"Wait!" she called after him. "I'm…" He stopped, but he didn't turn around. "I'll get you some dog food."

"Leave it in the bunkhouse."

Del walked away muttering, "The hell with her," to the dog. If she was interested, the woman heard him. If she wasn't, a little curse didn't matter to her anyway. But he was pretty sure he still had her attention, pretty damn sure he was getting under her skin right now.

"And we both know there's more'n one way to skin a cat," he whispered to his new companion. "Ain't that right?" Then he laughed at himself for conjuring an image of peeling Lila's T-shirt over her head. "Skin the cat" was one of his dad's crazy sayings.

"The hell with her" was not.

Del found Frank cleaning a saddle in the new barn. One wall of the tack room was lined with racks stocked with saddles and hooks heaped with bridles, all in beautiful condition. Frank was a true horseman.

"Brad back yet?"

"Haven't seen him." Frank tapped the lid on a can of saddle soap. "He took his pickup. I don't think he was too serious about checking cows. Not from a pickup."

"The fence was down about a mile off the highway on the cut-across. All three strands cut."

Frank dropped the can into a rubber tub. "Could be kids."

"There were tire tracks. I don't know why kids would go to all that trouble, though. Not the best place for a party. Nothing left behind. No cans, no bottles, no butts."

"Did you fix it?"

"For now. Should be replaced."

"You rode the fence line on horseback?" The older man's face lit up. "There's wire out in the shop. We'll load some up, drive over and do it right."

"I can take care of it now. Just say the word."

"I did. It's *we*. We'll go out and stretch some wire." He slid his stool up against the wall, lifted his John Deere cap, raked his fingers through thinning gray hair and then settled the cap back in place as though they were heading for town. "I think I'm gonna like you, Del. Seems like you're here to work."

"I've worked for guys who want me to wade right in and do what needs doing and guys who want me to wait for orders. I'm good either way."

Frank clapped a sturdy hand on Del's shoulder. "Then you'll be good loading up the wire in case my wife looks out the window. I'll bring the pickup around."

"Guess I'm done waiting."

The chance to spend quality time with Frank fit nicely into Del's plan, and considering the way things were working around the Flynn place, it had come sooner than expected. It was a good sign, he thought, and then he dismissed the idea. He was looking to connect the dots. From his perspective they were neither good nor bad. They were just dots. The connections were all that counted.

"I didn't mean to bother you with this," he told Frank as they approached the stretch of fence he'd patched earlier. He pointed, and Frank pulled over. "Retirement must be nice."

"Brad says I'm retired?" Frank chuckled. "Don't worry. You can answer truthfully. It won't get back to him."

"I guess what he said was, he's trying to get you to take it easy."

"In my old age?"

"Now, he didn't *say* that. You've got a real nice place here, Frank. Probably been building it up acre by acre for…"

"Most of my life." Frank pushed his door open, but he wasn't in any hurry to get out. He was taking in the view. Grass and sky. "Belonged to my wife's family, my first wife. I own half the land. Lila's grandmother left her the other half, along with the home place." He turned to Del, as though he was about to deliver news that deserved special treatment. "My first wife died."

"When Lila was twelve."

Frank raised his brow. "Brad told you?"

"Lila did. My mother died young, too."

Frank gave a tight-lipped nod. Del read the message in his eyes. Tough break all around.

"Lila's never forgiven me for getting married again. She should've outgrown that by now. A man doesn't stop living just because his wife dies. Especially not if he has a young child. Your dad remarry?"

Del shook his head. "Never did."

"Is that some kind of tradition?

"You mean for Indians?" Del shook his head. "My mother was white. My dad was Lakota. I'm sure he had his reasons for not getting married again, but being Lakota wasn't one of them."

"It's hard, losing your wife sudden like that. Or your mother. Leaves a big hole right through your chest. The wind—" he gestured with a shivery hand "—whistles right through."

Del showed Frank the tire tracks, which, interestingly enough, didn't elicit much reaction. Del had to fish for it.

"Brad said neighbors have been losing cattle."

"Could be rustlers, I guess. There's been some rustling now and again lately, but it's mostly been tribal cattle. I don't lease any tribal land, so I stay out of their business, but I've heard rumors about the tribe being short quite a few cows." Frank turned his attention to the fence, but he kept talking as he examined Del's fix. "They say the ranch manager is a suspect. Old fella named Stan Chasing Elk. His daughter and mine were real close."

"Who's accusing him?"

"Mostly the tribal police, but I guess the tribal council is getting down on him. Anyway, that's what I've heard. As long as it's just the tribe's cattle, it's none of my business."

"Could be it's your business. You callin' the law on this?"

"If we're missing cows, you damn betcha. You did a nice job here, but we'll string up new wire." His tone shifted, as though he'd been asked to testify. "It ain't Stan. We go way back. Good man, Stan." He turned his attention to a passing cloud. "Stan the Man. Remember the baseball player?"

Del glanced at the cloud, half expecting to see a Stan or two up there, acknowledging Frank's memory with a thumbs-up.

Frank snapped out of his reverie with a chuckle. "Course not. That was a long time ago."

"Stan the Man Musial. One for the books, and I do read some. Musial said, 'When the pitcher's throwing a spitball, just—'"

"'—hit it on the dry side,'" they quoted in unison, and then they both laughed as Frank clapped a hand on Del's shoulder.

"I played baseball in high school. First base. Pretty good hitter." Del read approval in Frank's face, and he figured the old man had faced more spitballs over the years than he had. "Your sport, too?"

"Was. Never had time to play much, but…" He looked down at the tire tracks and shook his head. "Yeah, I think we might've lost some cows. We'll see what Brad comes up with. I keep my books on paper. He's got this computer thing going, and we don't always match up."

"I'm not much of a computer guy myself."

"Glad I'm not the only one. Guess we need to get with the program, buddy." Chuckling, he laid his hand on Del's shoulder. "They say everybody's replaceable these days. Even cowboys."

"Yeah, that horse is out of the barn."

"Come to think of it, they haven't made the computer yet that can chase that horse down and run him back in."

"Or string wire," Del said. "So I guess I'm not completely replaceable."

"Brad either chose well or lucked out this time." Frank smiled. "I admire a man who knows the value of a good horse. Still the best way to herd cows."

* * *

Del tried two hills before he found a piece of high ground where his phone quit cutting out. Truth be told, he was one hell of a space-age cowboy. While truth telling wasn't part of his job description, he made an effort to keep mental tabs on it, and taking his smartphone in hand and tapping out a couple of texts allowed him to get in touch with reality even as he was keeping his head in the game. The message that came back was unsatisfying, but at least it was a contact.

Follow Benson. Get a line on Chasing Elk. Move up the line ASAP.

ASAP wasn't Del's preferred approach to a job. Space-age aside, a dyed-in-the-hide cowboy didn't do ASAP. If the question was "Fast or good?" his answer was always "The best you've ever had."

Which made him think of Lila.

"I like her," he told the dog in the passenger seat. He gave the animal's head a vigorous scratching, the velvety drop ears a floppy workout. The pup lifted his head, eyes closed in pure bliss. "Okay, so she rejected you for now, but it's not personal. She can't give up too soon. It would be like saying out with the old, in with the new. That's hard for a woman like her. She's got no ASAP button. Give her time."

The dog whined.

"No? Sorry, buddy, we got no choice. We gotta let her come to us. Okay?" He patted the dog's back. "Meanwhile, I'm here for you."

Chapter Three

"I think we're missing six head of steers," Brad reported. He glanced at Del as though he might have something to with it. Then he turned his attention to Frank, but he didn't look him in the eye. He dug his boot heel into the pulverized corral dirt like a kid who was having trouble making stuff up as he told his father how he'd done exactly what he was supposed to do. "Unless they got in with the cows. I mean, I drove across the south pasture and didn't see any steers in with the cows there. That's the only place…" He jerked up his chin suddenly. "You say there's tire tracks?" he asked Del. "What kind?"

"Sixteen and a half inch, probably a GM, maybe

a Ford—big one-ton sucker—towing a gooseneck trailer."

"What color?" Frank asked, straight-faced as hell.

"The pickup or the gooseneck?"

"Either one," Frank allowed. "Hell, both."

Del's expression matched the old man's. "Black. Had to be a matched set."

Brad was speechless, waiting for something to drop—a shoe, a net, something. Del purely enjoyed the seconds that passed before Frank tapped his shoulder with the back of his hand, signaling it was time for a good laugh.

"I can read tracks, but not quite that good," Del said.

"Ground's too dry," Frank said. "You were doing real good finding any tracks at all." He turned to Brad. "You sure we're missing six? You got ear-tag numbers?"

"Dad, they're *missing*."

"You get the numbers that are there," Frank explained with exaggerated patience. "The ones that aren't there are the ones we're looking for."

Brad glared briefly at Frank and then at the fence wire in the back of Frank's pickup. "You know, I told Del to get that fence fixed." He turned to Del. "You didn't need to go to my dad for help."

"He didn't," Frank said. "He was looking for you.

I went out there with him because I needed to get out of the damn house."

"Well, good. That's good." Nodding, Brad slid Del a cold glance. "I'll give the sheriff a call, tell him where to meet up so he can see what's going on out there." He turned back to Del. "You go get the tag numbers off those steers out where I showed you yesterday. You remember how to get there?"

"You don't want him to show you where he found the tire tracks?" Frank asked.

"You said the cut-across, right? How far off the highway?"

"Little less than a mile. I marked the fence with a red flag. You can tell where it was cut. Anyway, Sheriff Hartley can tell." Frank turned to Del. "I'll get us the list of tag numbers. We'll go out and check them off, see what's missing."

"You're not thinking about getting on a horse," Brad challenged.

"I think about it all the time."

"Don't tell Mom that. She's thinking all the time, too. About that trip you promised her after you get your other new knee." Brad sidled up to Frank. "Let me take care of this, Dad. We'll check the ear tags and figure out what's what. You get hold of Hartley. Better you than me." He looked over at Del and went back to being boss. "Mount up. Dad knows best."

* * *

Del let his horse drop back to a trot when he heard the roar of the pickup at his back. He didn't need help with taking ear-tag inventory—he could easily handle Frank's metal clipboard himself—and he doubted he would get much. But making waves didn't suit his purpose. Neither did ignoring Brad, as much as he wanted to. They both knew how many steers were missing. Brad didn't know or care which ones they were. But Frank cared, and that was another good sign.

Sign. Just a piece of information. *Connections, Fox. That's all you're looking for.*

"This works out better," Brad called out from the pickup.

Del slowed to a walk. "What does?"

"Letting Frank be the one to deal with the sheriff. I had a few run-ins with Hartley back when I was a kid, young and dumb. But I've stayed away from him since then. I need to keep it that way."

"I hear you." And hearing was enough. He kept his eyes on the view. Clear blue sky and rolling hills. The grand scheme. "Cops have tunnel vision. Out of sight, out of mind."

"You know it. I didn't count, but I figure there was probably a hundred head of steers in that pasture. Frank won't be satisfied until he has ear-tag numbers. There's no way around it."

"Don't worry about it. I'll take care of it."

"That's what I like to hear."

Brad came to a stop and toyed with the accelerator. Power. Play. Del spun his horse and let him prance a little in response.

"But you can't fake it," Brad warned. "He still keeps records."

"He seems pretty sharp."

"He's slipping. A year or two ago he wouldn't trust me to count the eggs in the fridge. So you got this?"

Del spun again, enjoying the buckskin's responsiveness, but a hint of something black lying in the shade of a chokecherry bush caught his eye. He urged his mount to trot ahead.

Brad shouted out to him and then followed, but he had to slow down for rutted terrain. By the time he reached the copse of bushes, Del had dismounted, dropped a knee to the ground and greeted the little corpse by name. Only the soft black hair moved, ruffled by the breeze.

"You got something I can wrap him up in?" Del asked when the sound of footsteps interrupted his thoughts. This wasn't the way you wanted to find the friend of a friend.

"Just leave him. I'll tell her there wasn't much left."

Del got up and craned his neck for a look in the pickup bed. "A plastic bag or something? When we get back to the barn I'll find something better to put him in."

"It's a dead dog, for God's sake. Coyotes should've made short work of the thing by now."

"They didn't." Del pulled his hat brim down to block out the sun. Or, far more irritating, the sight of Brad Benson. "She said she wants him back no matter what. It's a small thing to ask."

"Throw it in the back of the pickup. What's the use of having coyotes around if they don't do their part?" Brad gave him a look, half suspicious, half mocking. "Fox, huh? Maybe you're the coyote."

"Yeah, maybe."

It bothered him all afternoon. He worked around the steers as quickly as he could, taking care not to disturb them too much while he took inventory, but he thought about that dog the whole time. Thought about Lila. Thought about the fact that her damn stepbrother had no respect for anything that mattered, and that her affection for her dog mattered in a way that not much else in Del's own world did.

Except the job. His *real* job. Starting out, the job had meant freedom. It had meant reporting only to one person instead of a dozen. It had meant eating what he wanted, going to bed when he felt like it. It had meant out with the old and in with the new. He wasn't going to miss any of the old, and the new was yet to be discovered. But affection hadn't figured in anywhere. His father was gone, and Del couldn't help but think he'd died of a broken heart, that his affection for his son had become such a heavy burden that his big heart had cracked. And with his father's death a chunk of Del's own life had been removed, like some kind of surgical amputation. What he had—what there was for him to build on—was a strange and unexpected job.

Which had nothing to do with putting the lid on the small pine box he'd fashioned, hoping it would bring some kind of comfort to the woman who was going to miss the old dog he'd put inside.

"Wondered where you were."

Del closed his eyes and stifled a groan.

"You missed supper. What's… You got that dog in there?" Brad came too close for Del's comfort to the two sawhorses that supported the little casket like a crude catafalque. "Nice box. Where'd you find it?"

"I made it."

"That quick? You're a man of many talents, Fox." Brad ran his hand over the unfinished pine. "Where'd the wood come from?"

"Frank said I could help myself to the scrap pile."

"When I hired you, did I mention you'd be working for me?"

"You did." If Brad got a splinter, it would be Bingo's revenge. He'd treated the dog's body like roadkill.

"You got a question, I want you to come to me with it."

"You got work you want done, I want you to tell me." He smiled. He liked the way Brad had to look up to meet his eyes. "I didn't ask. He offered."

"You didn't seem like such a charmer when you hired on, but it sure didn't take you long to get all up in my family business." Brad pointed a finger. "You report to me, and I report to Frank." He came dangerously close to poking that finger into Del's chest. "And Lila's off-limits." Then he came to his senses and lowered his ridiculously soft hand.

"You tell me what you want done, I'll put in a full day's work and then some. You tell me who I can and can't talk to, I'll be leaving before the day's over." Del raised a brow. "And we both know you need me more than I need this job."

"Hey," Brad said quietly, palms raised in surrender. "Let's just, you know, step back from the edge here. I can tell you're a good hand. I see that already. And yeah, like they say, good help is hard to find." He leaned on the casket. "I'm a little touchy about my family. I've got a lot on my plate these days."

"Try taking smaller helpings." Del cast a disapproving look at the hand on the box.

"Yeah, you're right. I take on too much." Brad quickly folded his arms. "Now that you're on board, I'm gonna leave the haying up to Frank. He likes to run the machinery, but we gotta make sure he doesn't do much more than that. He won't even use the AC in the John Deere." He shrugged, as if to say, *What're ya gonna do?* "So why don't you go check in with Frank. Tell him as long as he's puttin' up hay, breakfast to dinner you're all his." Brad picked up the box. "While I deliver this little gift to Lila."

Del watched his "boss" walk out of the barn with the small casket under his arm. He told himself Brad was right. He needed to leave Lila alone. He knew better than to confuse himself for anybody's friend. What he'd just done had crossed the line.

"Like this."

Lila demonstrated the fingering on her plastic recorder for the umpteenth time. And for the ump-teenth time little Denise jumped in and played the tune start to finish before Rocky could get two notes in edgewise.

"Let's try it this way," Lila said. "Rocky plays the first three notes by himself." Lila demonstrated. "And then Denise has the next three notes by her-self. They're just the same at the first three. So it's…" No sooner had Lila put the instrument to her lips than Denise started tweedling. "A little too fast," Lila said.

"But it's right."

"The notes are right, but you're going too quickly. It's, 'Hot cross buns. Hot cross buns,'" Lila sang, demonstrating the tempo. "And then the next part—" The four-year-old beat her teacher to the tweeter once again. "That's good, a little closer than the first time, but not quite—"

All heads turned as Brad's pickup interrupted the front porch music lesson.

"He's driving across the yard again," Denise complained. "He shouldn't be doing that."

Lila shook her head slightly as the red short box pulled up only a few feet from the porch steps. Brad liked to make an entrance, and she had a feeling this one was part of some production she could do without. He got out, whacked the door shut, adjusted his jeans and strode around the front of the pickup as though he was there on official business.

"I wanna swing," Rocky said quietly.

"Lila doesn't like you driving across the yard," Denise called out.

"Sorry, I forgot." Brad propped his booted foot on the second porch step. "You got a minute?" he asked Lila.

"This one is taken." She smiled. She was nothing if not a good role model. "I should have one soon. What do you need?"

"I brought you something." He glanced at the kids. "It's after six. Where are the parents?"

"On their way."

"I wanna swing," Rocky repeated.

"I'm with you." Brad gave Rocky a thumbs-up. "Why don't you let them jump on the swings?"

"Go ahead." She held out her hand. "I'll take care of the recorders. We'll get it down pat tomorrow so we can put on our show next week." The two children couldn't drop their recorders and take off fast enough.

Lila set the plastic instruments aside and approached the pickup. She could see the kids from there.

She could also see the small box in the short box. "It's Bingo, isn't it?"

"'Fraid so. I found him in the south pasture, tucked up under a chokecherry bush."

She already had lowered the tailgate and pulled the box onto it. The lid was tied on with a length of soft cotton rope. She reached for one of the ends.

"You don't wanna do that."

"No, I don't." She slipped the half hitch. "But I have to make sure."

"You don't believe me?"

She didn't care about him. Her best friend lay still in a wooden box, cushioned on folded, well-worn denim within a nest of fresh hay.

"Hoo-wee!" Brad yowled. "Hard to get past the smell. That's why I said—"

"It's okay," Lila said. Alfalfa brought the scent of summer, and the smell of pine attested to newly sawn wood. She touched her friend's soft fur and discovered dampness. She couldn't tell whether there had been blood or bites or broken bones. Her friend might have been asleep except for the fact that he didn't lift his head and greet her hand with his wet nose and smooth tongue. She pulled the clip from her hair, making sure a few strands came with it. She liked it because it was shaped like a Milk-Bone. "And Bingo was his name-o," she whispered as she placed the clip inside the box.

"Damn," Brad said softly. "Hey, I'm sorry, Lila."

She looked up, puzzled.

"Really. I know how much he meant to you."

He didn't know, but he was trying to, at least for the moment. She would give him that. She didn't believe Brad had found him, picked him up and brought him back home, and there was no way he'd prepared the dog for burial.

"I'd dig a hole for him, but I'm supposed to be someplace right now." He looked up the road. "Here come the Vermillions."

Lila couldn't laugh any more than she could cry right now, and she wasn't sure which way she would go if her brain hadn't gone numb. But it was either very funny or awfully sad that her stepbrother had no idea how transparent he was.

"Denise's mom." Quickly she put the lid back on the box and grabbed the loose ends of rope. "I'm going to put him in the library for now. Would you...?"

"Yeah. Glad to." He waved to the oncoming

car, and then turned and made a megaphone of his hands. "Hey, kids! Somebody's mom is here."

Del found the nameless black pup waiting for him when he opened the door. He could tell his bed had been appropriated by a small body with black hair, but otherwise a double dose of scratching with a hearty "good dog" was in order. After the day he'd had, he welcomed the feel of the living, breathing, squirming dog in his hands. He figured Brad had helped Lila bury her own dog—why else would he hijack the remains?—and she probably wasn't in the mood for a canine visitor just yet. But on his very first off-leash walk, Not Bingo took off. Sure enough, he followed his nose for excitement and discovered Lila digging a hole smack in the middle of her garden.

Damn Benson for not taking care of that for her.

"Can I help you with that?" Del called out. The pup was already sniffing around the dirt pile, looking to answer the question for himself.

"I'm almost finished." She tossed a shovelful of South Dakota clay past the peak of the pile, and Not Bingo chased it.

Del eyed the box—somebody had retied his knot—and then peered into the hole. "That's pretty deep."

"I know." She leaned on the shovel, brushed away

a strand of hair with the back of her other hand. "I have a plan."

"You're gonna plant something over him?" He took hold of her free arm by the wrist and turned it palm up. Two blisters were blooming there. "Where are your gloves?"

"I wasn't thinking about my hands except…" She curled her fingers over her palm as though he'd caught her red-handed. "I don't like to wear gloves when I work in the garden. I like the feel of the dirt."

He reached for the shovel, and she released it to him. He dropped the blade into the hole and pushed hard on the handle.

"Thank you," she whispered. He glanced over his shoulder. From the sound of her voice he expected tears, but there were none. Sad eyes, wistful smile. She glanced at the pup—big help, digging in the dirt pile—and her face brightened a bit. But only momentarily, as she turned her attention back to the small pine box. "He looks comfortable in there. Like he just curled up and went to sleep. Could you tell what happened?"

"Just what you said. He found a shady spot, laid his tired body down and went to sleep."

"Why did you clean him up?"

He added dirt to the pile. "Figured you'd open up the box to say your goodbyes and he'd want to be looking his best."

"You're the one who found him, aren't you?"

"We were out checking for…" He paused in his digging so he could look her in the eye. She wanted details. He wanted to oblige. "Yeah, I found him." He drew a deep breath, trying to sort through the details and find words. "Didn't look like he'd been messed with at all. Not before or after. He looked peaceful."

She thought about it for a moment, as if she was forming a picture she wanted to keep. She looked him in the eye, nodded once and almost smiled. "I owe you a pair of jeans, don't I?"

"Nope. They were ready for retirement."

He dug until she told him to stop, squared up the bottom of the hole and they buried the box. She'd put up a good front until the hole was filled. Now she was making a point to turn her face without turning her back on him, but he could see her tears. The worst of it was she didn't make a sound. He wanted to do something, the right thing, the thing she needed, and he felt like putting his arms around her. But he knew she wasn't ready.

The pup knew it, too. He'd grabbed himself a cool patch of grass and sat quietly, but he was tuned in, waiting for a signal. He was all eyes and ears. All the woman had to do was glance his way.

She knew it, just like the pup did, and just like the pup, she held back. "Have you named him?"

"Nope. Waiting for you."

"No, he's yours. He likes me all right, but he

picked you. I called the vet. He'll be making a call at one of the neighbors on Monday, so he's going to stop by."

"I'll pay his bills and everything, but I don't…" Del sighed. It was a bunch of hooey. *He picked you.* Beggars couldn't be choosers, neither man nor beast. "He picked the wrong guy."

"I don't think so. They know." She brushed her hands together, winced a little, and that was his signal.

He took her hands in his, turned her palms up and made a sympathetic sound deep in his throat. "I've got something for this." He looked up and smiled, then let one hand go so he could brush a glittering tear from her cheek with the tip of a finger while he tucked her other hand against his chest. "I'm no stranger to blistered hands."

"No." She pressed her trembling lips together for a moment, and he expected to be turned away. The evening breeze lifted a hank of hair and wrapped it across her eyes. She tossed her head and gave him a sad smile. "No, you wouldn't be."

He put his arm around her shoulders, and they walked to the bunkhouse, where he threw his hat on the wooden chair as he ushered her to the bathroom. She stood in front of the sink and started to turn on the water, but he reached around her and beat her to the faucet handles. He stole a glance at the mirror. Her eyes were closed, lashes wet, cheeks shiny. His chest felt tight. He wished she'd just let go, let the dam bust wide-open. But it was her call.

He left the door open and the light off. The shadows gave her privacy. It was a small room, barely space for one, so he sat on the can, took Ivory soap in his hand and gently washed her blistered palms. Her hands were steady, but her shoulders shuddered, and her breath quivered almost imperceptibly. She was holding on by a thread, trusting him with her broken skin. He felt privileged.

He blotted her hands dry and took her to his bed, where he sat her down and squatted on his heels beside her knees so he wouldn't be on the bed with her. All the touching and caretaking was making him feel randy as hell.

He took a flat, round snuff can from the nightstand drawer. It was one of the cans his father had used for the all-purpose remedy that had gotten Del through blisters, burns and scrapes over the years. He'd never seen his father chew snuff, but he always had a stash of empty cans.

"This stuff is magic," he promised as he dipped his finger into the old can and dabbed the salve on her blisters. "My dad used to make it. He used it on any kind of wound, any kind of hide, skin, whatever living thing that could get hurt. I used to say, 'Dad, you're in the wrong business. You could sell this stuff and make a fortune.'"

"What...business?" She took a breath between words. Her voice was heavy.

"Cattle. Horses. Nothing like what you've got here, but we got by. Like most small..." She made an unrestrained sound. Finally. A little whimper that might've come from the pup. Del's heart raced, but his hands moved slowly, carefully applying the salve, and he kept his eyes on the road map laid out in the creases of her palms. "It only stings at first. Dad called it heals-quick. 'We'll put some heals-quick on it,' he'd say. And then he'd..." Del blew gently, filling her hands with the air he'd taken in. He wanted to be magic. It was a foolish thought, but he wanted to be—just for a moment—anyone but who he was. Undercover, he'd been playing an assigned role so long—an alter ego, maybe—that he didn't know who Delano Fox really was anymore. And until this moment he'd been fine with that.

In another moment he would be fine again.

Unless he did the stupid thing, which, of course, he did.

He looked up and got lost in her eyes.

Lila lifted her gaze from his rough and gentle hands to the lush black-brown hair that angled across his forehead. She wanted to touch it, but she didn't want to discourage him from tending to her hands. Funny. She was generally given to taking care of herself. She didn't like feeling needy.

But maybe that wasn't what she felt. His touch, his breath on her skin, his undivided attention, it was all good. It felt like kindness getting its arms around sadness. She willed him to look up and let her see this wondrous thing in his eyes. And when he did, the feeling came full circle. It was mutual. It was an electrical charge, a living spark. She smiled a little through unshed tears.

He smiled a lot. "Better?"

She nodded.

"Asap."

She questioned him with a crinkled brow. He opened his mouth to explain, but the dog startled them both by leaping onto the bed, tail wagging.

"How's that for a name? It just came to me. Him and me, we had a conversation about his situation. We got all philosophical about timing and possibilities."

"Asap," she echoed, nodding.

"It's one of those names that strikes you as smart-ass—me anyway—but when you think about it, there's two sides to the ASAP story. Soon, but not rushed. Good is possible, but so is not so good." His eyes held her gaze as he pressed the lid back on the can and tossed it past her onto the bed. "Did I mention my father was Lakota? Or had you figured that out?"

"Neither. You didn't, and I didn't, not exactly." She touched his chin with her fingertips, traced the angle of it, felt its surprising smoothness. "But I wondered. You're beautiful."

"So are you."

He slid his arm around her shoulders, nestled her nape in the crook of his elbow and drew her to him for a sweet kiss, a tender greeting eagerly met. With the touch of his tongue he bade her to part her lips and taste his beauty, let him taste hers, and she did, and he made her want more. If she took him in her arms she could have more. He nibbled her lips playfully, changed the angle of their kiss and made it harder and deeper and wetter, and then he made it soft and sweet again. A needy sound threatened to escape her throat, but she held it back. It was such a pathetic thing, it tucked its tail and mercifully retreated.

He knew. He touched his forehead to hers and whispered, "Not possible." And then he amended, "Or maybe just too soon."

Chapter Four

Bucky's Place was about the last place Del wanted to be, which was a sure sign he'd lost focus. The truth was, Bucky's was exactly where he needed to be. The atmosphere was right for getting his head back into the game. Meeting the locals was a necessity. He had to give most of the jokes at least a chuckle, drink no more than one beer for every three Brad was putting away—same for winning at pool, no more than one round out of three—match the names up with the attitude and file it all away. Some people just begged to get robbed. Others looked for times and places to oblige them.

Bucky's was the right place for the confluence of the first with the second.

"Looks like them rustlers are back," a voice at the end of the bar announced. Taylor Rhoades. Del had him in the "comedian" file. "The Blaylocks just lost a dozen head."

"Yeah, we lost six," Brad said. "Steers," he added. "Was it cows they took from Blaylock or steers?"

"Pretty sure he said steers. Cow-calf operations, they're probably safe this time of year. Steers are a helluva lot easier to move."

"You heard about Stan Chasing Elk, didn't you?" Carl Schrock offered. Carl's input was worthy of a mental file. His wife was the hometown hairdresser, which made him privy to all kinds of local lore. Whether it was thirdhand, secondhand or straight from the horse's mouth, talk was news in a town like Short Straw.

"He selling off tribal cattle again?"

"They never proved that," Carl reminded anyone listening. "You ask me, it was Chet Klein. After they fired him from that ag program at the college, suddenly the whole rustling epidemic kinda died down."

"Sounds like it's flared back up again," Taylor said.

"Maybe never really died, you know?" Brad speculated. "If a guy's got any kind of insurance…"

"They don't pay out until every last form is filled out and all the official noses have smelled every armpit in the county." Taylor wasn't speaking from experience. He drove truck for the Short Straw Co-Op.

"Who's going to the VFW shindig this weekend?" Brad asked. "I hear they're bringing in a live band. All the way from Pierre is what I hear."

"Could be a line from their theme song. 'They got a band from Pierre, that's what I hear,'" Taylor crooned.

Carl groaned. "Taylor used be in the church choir till they kicked him out for singing."

"All he really wanted was the robe," Brad said with a grin.

"And I never gave it back, neither."

"They didn't want it back after they found out you wore it on Halloween, buck naked underneath."

"How'd they find out?" Del asked.

"He flashed the choir director." Carl flipped open his denim jacket as he spun his bar stool full circle.

"Mooned," Taylor protested above the whoops and whistles. "And she told my ol' lady, which is why we don't go to dances no more. I keep telling her, ain't no way we'd run into that woman at a dance."

"You going, Carl?" Del asked.

"You damn betcha. They've got my wife selling tickets to her hair customers. Those old soldiers know how to round up the troops. Just give every woman a book of tickets and tell her it's all for charity."

And so went the boys' night out.

Mental notes neatly filed, Del figured on calling his badge-carrying contact on his way back to the Flynn place, but Brad jumped into the passenger seat just as he threw the truck into Reverse. "You'll have to bring me back for my pickup in the morning." Brad nodded toward Main Street. "Sheriff just drove past. You don't drink much, do you?"

Del draped his arm over the back of the bench seat and looked over his shoulder. Story of his life. "I can take it or leave it."

Brad slid down in the seat. "I sure hit the jackpot when I hired you."

"You going to this dance?"

"Not if I don't have to. And since I'm not married or otherwise tied down, I don't have to. I might stop in and check it out, but if the band sucks I'll find another party." He glanced sideways. "You?"

"Lila doesn't seem to get out much."

"She doesn't want to." Brad chortled. "Go ahead and ask her. See what she says. Bet you fifty bucks she says no."

"Ain't much of a bettin' man."

"He don't drink, and he don't gamble. With so damn much to recommend you, it's funny you're not married, Fox. Women love cowboys."

"That's because we're lovable. You want marriageable, you're looking for a whole different breed."

The lights were on in the old schoolhouse that stood within a few yards of Lila's place. As late as it was, Del figured he ought to check out the place, see what was going on, make sure she was okay. *Quietly*, if he could manage it. The heavy door threatened to give him away, but he kept the squeak to a minimum and slipped into the entry, clearly once a mudroom. A list headed Library Rules was posted above a row of metal coat hooks. "Honor the honor system. Sign the guest book. Book donations welcome."

She called those rules?

Lila was sitting on the floor, back to the door, hunched over whatever she was working on. If the pup was studying for guard duty, he was asleep on the job.

"Are you—"

They yelped and jumped, woman and dog both, like a pair of jack-in-the-boxes.

"—open?" Del squatted, butt to boot heels. "Get over here, Asap. The idea is to jump up *before* the dirty crook makes you look." He scratched the wiggly pup's chest. "Dog ears never sleep, Ace."

"Oh, look what you made me do." She'd dripped

black paint on her work in progress. "Made me more than look, you dirty crook."

"Sorry about that. I figured this time of night it might be an actual crook. What are you making? A sign?" Pretty obvious—it said Free Library—and she told him as much with a wide-eyed glance. "I thought maybe this place was for the kids. Where you teach them, or whatever you do in day care. Isn't it like nursery school?"

"Nursery school? What rock have you been living under? My day care is like preschool, only we don't have preschool around here, so people think of me as a babysitter. Which is okay, but I do teach. Even though I'm not certified, I sneak it in anyway.

"But this—" she gestured expansively, and with no shortage of pride "—is for everybody. Including sneaky crooks and hired hands. And kids, of course. I'm still working on it. People are beginning to stop in. The county used to have a bookmobile, but the funding was cut."

He surveyed the shelves. Most of them came up to his waist. He would have to crawl around on the floor to find a book. But he said, "This is great."

"My dad bought the schoolhouse for a dollar after they built the district school, the one I went to."

"He moved it here?"

"He did. Before I was born, so it's been here all my life. Dad said he bought it for storage, but he actually went to school here. One room for all the elementary grades. Don't you just love it?"

He meant merely to indulge her by taking a quick look around, but she was right. The place was enchantment in the making. The practical rancher had storage in mind, but his daughter had a better idea.

Del took a close look at the woodstove in the back of the room. "Is this original to the building?"

"Dad put that in when I started playing here. I claimed it by coming in here all the time, bringing toys in and leaving them here, putting my marks on the walls."

"Little squatter," he said with a smile.

"See those desks?" She pointed to a motley collection of old student desks in the back corner. "Whenever we ran into one on sale somewhere, Dad would buy it for me."

"Sounds like you were Daddy's girl."

"I always was, I guess. And for a while after my mother died, it was just us."

"Yeah," he said. "I know what that's like."

But she'd done better than he had. She'd made good, and the schoolhouse was only one example of the good things she'd put her mind to. It reminded him of a little town he'd visited on a school trip a very long time ago. It was a place out of time, a retreat.

A library.

There were two tall bookcases against one wall,

each shelf partially filled with books, and two waist-high shelving units in the middle of the open space that were crammed with what looked to be children's books. Each wall had its own color—red around the windows on the east wall opposed by solid black behind the old slate blackboard on the west, yellow surrounding the metal bookcases on the south and white backing the mudroom. Clearly, she knew something about his father's people besides the fact that they produced good-looking sons.

For the Lakota, the four directions were more than ritual symbols. They looked to the East for the rising red sun, which brought light, the mark of wisdom. West was black—the end of day, darkness and death—but it was also the home of Thunderbird, who brought rain to sustain life. Cold white North brought hard times, but it also offered cleansing, and yellow South's warm winds prompted growth and promoted life.

Del thought of Stan Chasing Elk, the man some suspected of stealing cattle. He hadn't met the man yet, but standing within four walls painted the colors of the four directions, he felt the need to clear him, lay all suspicions to rest. Strange feeling, since he wasn't a religious man, not the way his father had once been.

Hearing Lila talk about her father had him looking around for some kind of connection to his own. Hell, it was just paint.

"This used to be my playhouse," she was saying. "Play school, play castle, play store. Now it's my community contribution after we lost the bookmobile." She nodded toward the dog and questioned him with a silly frown. "Ace?"

Del shrugged.

"I know what you're up to," she said. "But an Ace doesn't replace a Bingo."

He laughed. "You're giving me way too much credit, woman. I'm not that clever." He signaled the pup. "Get over here, Asap." He flashed Lila a bright-eyed wink. "See how that works? Wagging his tail behind him."

"Hmm. Too cute by half. Both of you." She turned to her artwork, and he peered over her shoulder. She'd messed up the dot over the *i* in *Library*. "Now what am I going to do?"

"I got this." He took a knee, braced his left forearm and gestured for the brush. "Turn it into something else."

"No smiley faces," she warned.

"Not your style." He considered his options for a moment, then dipped the brush into the black paint and deftly turned the stray marks into an open book. "How 'bout that?"

"It's perfect." She turned a genuinely smiling face to him. "You have a good eye and a steady hand."

"Which make me the designated driver."

"For Brad and his buddies?"

"Just Brad. The man in charge."

"Do you really think so?"

"I went out in the field with Frank today. He tested me out on the mower before he let me run it. Then I got to knock down a patch of alfalfa while he raked the crested wheat he'd cut the other day. I love the smell of newly mown alfalfa. Frank says he's had trouble around it lately. Gets all stuffy."

Lila shook her head. "Brad is useless."

"He's the one who hired me, so I gotta say he has his good points. But Frank's the cattleman in this outfit."

"It's *his* outfit."

"And yours, right?"

Her tone became guarded. "I have a lease agreement with my father for the use of my land. That's all. It's my father's operation. He manages everything, keeps it afloat, feeds and waters, buys and sells, and he writes the checks. It'll be his name on your check, not Brad's, and definitely not June's." She arched an eyebrow. "Not yet anyway."

"Brad doesn't do much without running it by Frank, huh?"

Both eyebrows. "He didn't run you by Frank."

"But?"

"But maybe we got lucky. For once Brad was in the right place at the right time and hired, yes, maybe the right man." She studied his artwork. "Saturday night at Bucky's Place, right? You stopped in for what? Directions?"

He offered half a smile. "A little more than that."

"What more?"

"I wanted a drink. I *needed* a job."

"And there was Brad." She raised an eyebrow. "Fate works in mysterious ways."

"Sure does." He handed her the paintbrush and turned to the tall bookcases. "So what've we got here? You willing to trust me with a book?"

"I trust everyone with a book. I'm not always here, but the door's always open. So far I've found that the honor system brings out the best in people."

He chuckled, and he ran his finger along a row of book spines. "If I wasn't honor bound before you said that, I sure am now. Help me pick out a good Western."

"Check this box." She scooted a big carton across the floor. "The word's gotten out, and the donations have been pouring in. I'm running out of shelving."

"I can help you with that. There's plenty of good lumber in what your dad calls the scrap pile."

"You're a good carpenter," she said quietly.

"It won't be fancy. I'm a pretty good *rough* carpenter."

"I'll make you supper. It won't be fancy, but it'll stick to your…" She trailed off as he reached for her hands, turned them over and checked for signs of healing. "Ribs. It helped."

His gaze met hers. "What did?"

"Your dad's medicine. You." She smiled. "You helped."

"Dad and me. We'll take you up on your offer. We could both stand to put some meat on our ribs, but especially Dad. Bony as hell, that guy." Poor Lila looked stricken. He indicated the walls with a gesture. "You've honored the colors of the four directions here. You know about sharing your food with the *wanagi*, don't you? Feed the spirits?"

"I thought you were supposed to honor the dead." She chided him with a look. "Bony as hell?"

"Graveyard humor." He shrugged. "Closely related to Indian humor. But feeding the spirits is no joke."

"Okay."

He smiled. "I'd like to come for supper. But there's something I'd like more." He tucked his thumbs in his belt. "I'd like to take you to the dance this weekend."

"Dance?" Stricken again.

"At the VFW." He put her hands on his shoulders, slipped his arms around her waist. "I get to hold you like this. You get to hold me. We get to sway to the music. Don't know what kind—some band from Pierre."

"A live band?"

"So they tell me. Fund-raiser for the VFW. Support our troops." He drew her hips close to his and swayed slightly, slowly, side to side. "Dance with me," he whispered.

She lifted her chin, he lowered his and they met halfway. He kissed her eagerly, licking her lips apart, seeking her tongue, stealing her breath, and she held nothing back. She pressed her fingers into his shoulders, kneaded him there, made him imagine her working him over, shoulders to soles and all points in between. He made a promise to himself in that moment that they would get there, and he lowered his head to deliver his promise to her slender neck and her velvety earlobe. She trembled in his arms.

Del rocked her, hip to hip, and, oh, yeah, there was music playing inside his head. He glanced down at the floor behind her and realized they were being watched. Asap tipped his head to one side, all big eyes and cocked ears. Del laughed.

"I'm not much of a dancer," Lila said. She started to pull away, but he was having none of that. "Because I tend to stiffen up," she added quickly.

She wasn't the only one.

"Got a radio?" He nuzzled her hair. "We could use a little easy-does-it music."

"Even without music, you move like the ocean," she whispered.

"Because I'm not thinking about it." He slid his hands down, spread them high on her bottom. Her jeans felt loose enough that he was sure he could slip his hands under the waistband and fill them with her tight little ass. "Don't think."

"I can't afford—" She pressed her cheek against his. "I like you too much."

"That's a bad thing?"

"It could be. I don't know what you're up to."

"I'm trying to get a date for the dance. I asked. I tried out, didn't step on any toes." He backed off gradually and looked her in the eye. "Did I?"

She smiled and shook her head.

"You move like a natural woman. You didn't stiffen up at all."

She gave him a naughty smile. "*You* did."

"I'm a natural man." He sat on the desk, took her hands in his and drew her to stand between his spraddled legs. "A man who's wondering what it's gonna take to get an answer."

"That kiss is still working on me."

"Here comes its reinforcement." A tug on her hands brought her lips within reach of his.

This time their kiss was like frosting on the cake—smooth and playful, topping off a welcome temptation.

He opened his eyes slowly and found her licking her sweet bottom lip. "Yes?"

"Yes. And the bookshelves…" She took a seat beside him and surveyed the empty wall space. "You don't have to do that. That's extra work, and I can't…" She gave her head a tight shake. "Thanks, but the truth is, I'm just glad you're here to help Dad. Lately we've had some hired men who were more trouble than they were worth."

"I don't mean to cause you any trouble at all." He squeezed her hand, and she turned to him, eyes bright with her willingness to taste more trouble. All he wanted was another taste of her, which was no trouble. Not for him anyway. Not unless thinking made it so.

"Oh, Del, you…" She dropped her head back and laughed. "You have no idea."

"I don't know about that." He carried their clasped hands to his mouth and kissed the back of hers. "Do you have any ideas?"

"Call it a night before the sun beats us to it?" She raised an eyebrow. "Maybe get some sleep."

"Mmm, let's just sit here together and watch the paint dry."

She laughed.

"As soon as it's light out, I'll put the new sign up for you and take some measurements for the shelves. You got a tape measure?" She lifted her shoulder and he frowned, touched his fingertips to her temple and then slid them through the soft hair pulled back from her face. He imagined releasing the clip and unfurling her hair. "I'm not looking for anything in return. I'm donating. The sign says donations welcome."

"*Book* donations."

"I have a few paperbacks I can throw in." He eyed the existing bookcases and pictured them replaced with others of his construction. "How tall do you want them? They should all be the same. All wood. We can paint them, and I can bolt them to the wall." He caught her dubious look. "I like to keep busy."

"Brad will keep you busy."

He shook his head. "Give me a break. Bucky's Place is gonna get old real fast."

"I don't know what your agreement is, but don't let Brad tell you his hands work overtime. Most of them turn out to be next to useless."

"I won't. I'll do you proud on the shelving. I learned a lot helping my dad. Life skills, you know? Best father-to-son legacy there is. I'm a hands-on kind of a guy." He smiled and gave her hand a quick squeeze. "Trade-wise."

"But you like to read."

"I do now. Hated school when I was a kid. Hated being cooped up." He gave a dry chuckle. "I had no idea. Guess you're right. Ideas aren't my strong suit."

"I'm not gonna touch that one," she said with a smile.

"Aw, c'mon. Disagree with me." He stood and drew her to her feet. "Here's a simple one. How 'bout I walk you to your door? Unless you'd rather get complicated and walk me to mine."

"You can drop me off. Ace will see you the rest of the way. He's *your* dog. And it looks like he needs water." She glanced at the dog, whose tongue was lolling. "By the way, I fed him."

"So did I. Looks like he's working both sides." Del wagged his finger at Asap. "You've got us figured out, don't you?"

The pup jumped up and wagged his tail in response.

"I wish *I* did," Lila said as they walked to the door.

"You're trying too hard. Just go with the flow." They stepped out onto the plank platform that served as a stoop. "Would you look at that," Del said softly. Morning's first blush colored the horizon. "Here's an idea. Feed me, and I'll repay you with a few bookshelves."

Lila nodded toward the sawtooth silhouette underpinning the spread of an orange-red splash and the slow rise of gold rays. "After this." She turned to him as a flurry of birdcalls hastened sunrise, and he took her in his arms and kissed her thoroughly.

Chapter Five

With his phone to his ear, Del sat on his patient mount and watched a small herd of Double F cows graze the grassy draw below. He never knew where he might be able to get a cell signal, and he was apt to lose a signal as unexpectedly as he found it. He had to make the minutes count.

"My guess is Saturday night," he told his contact. "There's gonna be a big charity event, and most people will be in town. Benson's not too subtle about checking on the neighbors' plans. Could be he's just feeding information to whoever's calling the shots. If he makes a move, I'll play my next card. If not…"

"Have you run into Standing Elk yet?"

"Soon. He's a friend of a friend. That's the best way to gain access here. I know what I'm doing."

The sound of his own words suddenly hit him hard. He was telling the kind of loaded truth that always left a prickly feeling in his mouth. He'd been working both sides of Rustler Street for so long he knew every sign and every shortcut better than the residents—ranchers on one side, rustlers on the other. He was some of each—a trickster and a true mixed breed—which made him the right man for a job that rendered him the wrong man to be doing anything but that job. He was bound to it, and for good reason. He'd dug himself a hole, and the job was his lifeline. But it was a tightrope, a one-man wire. He could easily find himself back at the bottom of the hole. A good man would stay clear of anyone he felt tempted to get close to in a good way. If he took a fall, he could easily take her with him.

But instead of staying clear, he was taking her to a damn dance. He tried to tell himself that it just fit too perfectly into his plans and, really, as long as he didn't try to take it any further, what could it hurt? Besides, he'd just gotten his hair trimmed, bought a new shirt, shined up his boots—the whole nine yards.

So much for turning a trickster into a good man.

"Dad was really surprised when I told him I was going to the dance," Lila told Del as they headed onto the highway on date night. Midsummer's early-evening light was still bright, but it had gone nice and soft. "I thought he might decide to go, too, but June said no."

"She doesn't strike me as the stay-at-home type."

"She likes to go places, but she's not interested in Short Straw. It's drab. It's dull. The people are twenty years behind times. Harkin's Grocery doesn't sell her brand of yogurt. She'll drive all the way to Pierre for a loaf of bread." Lila leaned her head on the rest and turned toward him. He could feel the warmth of her easy attitude. They were friends now. "Dad isn't quite as old as he looks, and June isn't as young as she thinks she is."

"Your dad looks like a man who's worked hard all his life. I wouldn't want to guess how many years that's been. June seems like she's got one foot out the door. Kinda temporary."

"Like you?"

"I'm here for the job. A hired hand is always temporary. But while I'm here, I need to be part of the operation. Otherwise, why keep me on?"

"You are one wise cowboy. Is Brad going to this thing tonight?"

"He said he might check it out."

"Without his hired man? That's a surprise. Brad likes to show up with a sidekick. Makes him look important."

Del smiled at the road ahead. "Lots of surprises, and the night's still young."

Lila wished she had worn jeans. This was, after all, the Short Straw Activity Center, and a woman in a dress was a rarity. Blouses were ruffled or sheer or scoop neck—maybe all three—but there were no skirts. Tight jeans tucked into a pretty pair of boots was considered female finery.

There wasn't an unfamiliar face in the whole place, and she sorely wished they'd stop looking at her as though she'd just walked into the wrong bathroom. She tugged on the skirt of her silky soft-blue dress—it felt as though it was twisted somewhere—and looked up at Del when she felt his hand on the small of her back. He smiled, and nothing felt twisted anymore.

Which didn't stop the neck twisting their presence seemed to be causing. Unlike her stepbrother, Lila didn't want to get noticed, especially not as the unexpected guest, the woman who never left home. If people talked about her, speculated about her or, worst of all, pitied her, she didn't want to know about it.

"Lila!"

Oh, for Pete's sake, had Connie Vermillion forgotten seeing her just yesterday when she'd picked Denise up from day care? She hurried in Lila's direction, giving a window-washer wave.

"Lila, you're here. Good for you, honey. Jeez, I almost called to see if I could get you to take the kids tonight. Grandma isn't feeling well. But Jeanie decided to stay home tonight, so..." Connie sneaked a quick peek at Del and added, "Jeanie's my sister."

Lila introduced Del to her friend, who stared at him as though he was made of chocolate. "He's working for Dad," Lila supplied.

"I'm... My daughter goes to Lila's for... You're not from around here, are you?"

Del smiled and said he wasn't, and Lila thought surely Connie's gesturing and sputtering had to be uncomfortable for him, but it didn't show. Because he must get this kind of reaction all the time. He was the best-looking man in the room. And she was with him.

"Is the rest of the family here?" Connie asked, and it took Lila a moment to tune in.

"I'm, uh, I'm here with Del." And he was patiently carrying a big Tupperware bowl. She relieved him of it quickly. "Where should I put this? Just potato salad."

"I'll take it. You can never have too much potato salad." Connie took the bowl, turned and then re-turned. "It's good to see you, Lila. I mean, I just saw you, but it's good to see you *here*, out for a..." Her smile was outrageously wide. For Del. "Good chance to meet people."

"I've met a few." He scanned the room. "I see some familiar faces."

"You two have fun, okay?" Connie was blushing as she looked at Del, and she looked quickly away. "I like your dress, Lila. You look great."

"I should've worn jeans," Lila muttered as she watched pretty, petite Connie walk away.

"You kidding? You're turning heads."

"I know. And it's not the dress." She laughed. He was wonderful. "You'd think I didn't socialize. Ever." And maybe she didn't, but she used to. It wasn't as though she'd been in storage. She was disgusted with herself for feeling self-conscious. It wasn't fair to her date. They were on her home turf. She should be introducing him around.

But she wasn't ready. "Let's get a table."

"You see anyone you want to sit with?"

"Yes." She grabbed his hand and met his eyes. "Right here."

"How about that corner—"

"Perfect." Not a corner table, but the very end of a long table in the far corner of the room. Glasses of tasseled wheat served as decorations "Let's grab it."

"What would you like to drink?" he asked.

"I don't know. I haven't eaten much today."

"Then we'll get you something to eat. Where's the kitchen?"

"Oh, no. I'm fine. I should've sampled more potato salad. Are we early? These things never start on time. I'm just—" she hunched up her shoulders, gave a tight smile and told a little white lie "—ready to start dancing."

"Let's." He slipped his hand around hers. "How can I make this easier?"

She drew a deep breath, blew it out, looked up at him and smiled. "I'm good."

"Hey, Del, are those seats taken?" A friendly little guy with a firm paunch and farmer tan, Carl Schrock gestured with the Stetson he gripped by the point in the crease of the crown. Del waved him on over. "Good to see you, Lila." Carl toasted her with his hat before he clapped it on his head and pulled a slim, curly-haired blonde to his side. "Del, this is my wife, Darlene."

"We've met. Paid a visit to Dar's Downhome Dos today." Del took off his hat and plowed his fingers through his hair. "You did such a nice job, Dar, I should've left the hat off. Now I'm sportin' hat hair."

"Del bought my last pair of tickets, too," Darlene said. "Like I told him, he sure works fast. New to Short Straw, and already he's dating the homecoming queen."

Lila questioned Del with a look, and he lifted one shoulder. "She asked me who the other ticket was for. Royalty, huh? If I'd known that, I might not've had the nerve to ask." He turned back to Darlene. "Lila owed me a favor after I helped her with a sign for the library."

"No woman can resist doing a little charity," Carl said. "Right, Dar? Dar won the prize for selling the most tickets. What did we get, darlin'?"

"We got a flagpole. Last year I won the flag. First thing tomorrow we're going to get it all set up."

"We?" Carl poked his wife's arm as though checking for doneness. "Will you be digging the hole or mixing up the cement?"

"The library gets a sign, and my shop gets a flag. We're calling out to the people on the highway." Darlene used her hands to describe her plan. "We'll change our colors. We'll make a barber pole for the house and put up a new sign by the gate. Red, white and blue."

"We." Carl turned to Del and rolled his eyes.

"A theme," Darlene enthused. "I'll change the shop name from Downhome to All-American. Dar's All-American Dos." She turned to Lila. "Do you have the phone number on the library sign? You might get more customers if you put the phone number right on the sign."

"The library's free. I don't get customers. I wanted a sign on the schoolhouse so people would stop coming to the house."

"My shop's in the house. The basement. A barber pole to show where the door is, Carl. We have to put in a separate door anyway. I got another warning notice."

"See there. The damn hair police'll be coming for

us. You don't need any more attention, Dar. You've got enough customers." Carl grabbed a stalk of wheat from the table arrangement and held it like a pencil. "I priced it out. You know what an outside door into the basement would cost me? Even if I did it myself, it would—"

"We could hire Del," Darlene suggested. "He made the library sign."

"*I* made the library sign," Lila said. "He just—"

"We could hire Lila," Carl said with a grin.

"Lila has her own home business with a separate door. Right, Lila?"

"Yes, but I don't have a flag."

"You need a flag," Darlene said.

"Dar…" Carl said.

"It's a *library*." She slapped her husband's arm. "Lila definitely needs a flag."

"Sounds like you're in good with the VFW, Darlene. Maybe you can talk them out of another flag for Lila," Del suggested. "And maybe persuade them to get this party started."

"This is what they call the social hour," Darlene said. "Buy your drink tickets now, you get peanuts and pretzels—all you can eat."

"We gotta play short straw to see who's buying." Carl snatched several more stalks of wheat from the vase and snapped off the grain. "See, Del, this is always the table decoration in Short Straw. Built-in entertainment." He snapped one straw in half. "Who wants to draw first?"

Del reached across the table, but Lila slipped her hand over his elbow.

"You don't have to buy any—"

"I got paid today." He patted her hand. "Relax, okay?"

"Will you look who's here," Darlene whispered to the group. "Paula Rhoades. Taylor got to come to a dance. Whatever you guys do, if he starts acting crazy, don't egg him on."

The band started to play before the food was served. A few pretzels took the edge off Lila's hunger and a glass of white wine eased her nerves. After about half a glass the stuff actually tasted pretty good. The second half loosened her up for dancing. Del seemed to be nursing his beer, but he didn't need much loosening up. He had ball bearings in his hips, and his boots were made for dancing. Food was soon the furthest thing from Lila's mind. Somehow he made her body swing and sway, made her feet go the right way, and when she tripped herself up, he covered for her. He was a good time, and she was having it.

Until Brad showed up.

"You got her to come." He made a show of shoving a congratulatory hand in the direction of Del's gut. "What did we say? Fifty?"

Laughing, Del managed to avoid the handshake by countering with a friendly hand on Brad's shoulder. "Whatever you said, man, I wasn't listening. No harm, no foul, no debt."

"That's right. You had the inside track, and you passed it up." Brad eyed another couple on the dance floor. "Looks like Carl Schrock is having himself a fine time."

"His wife is this year's ticket-sales champion," Lila said as she linked arms with Del. He was her date. She was there with him, and yes, she wanted everyone to know it.

"Won the grand prize," Del added. "Seem like good people, the Schrocks."

"I like Carl." Brad watched for a moment, and then he turned away muttering, "Good man."

Del was having himself a damn good time. It was fun to watch Lila come out of her shell. They exchanged quips and shared laughs with the others who stood in line for the buffet. He had almost forgotten why he was really there—or maybe he'd almost changed his mind about it—when he noticed Brad was leaving.

"I'll be right back. Okay? Right back." He took a plate from the serving table and put it in Lila's hands. "Be sure you get enough to eat. We've got more dancing ahead of us."

He could feel her eyes boring into his back as

he pushed open the door. She hadn't asked earlier, hadn't said a word, just looked at him, all big blue eyes filled with confusion. He would explain. The moment would come, and he would tell her what he could and hope it was enough. But for now he had to take care of business.

There was no need to keep Brad's taillights in view. Del knew where he was headed. Only a few hours ago he'd gotten his hair cut there, and he'd noticed how many steers were grazing the pasture north of the house. Two miles down the road he found the hole cut in the fence.

They'd picked the right spot, the one he would have chosen himself. Clear, black velvet sky, moonless night, the draw was hidden from the road and there was a little hill for good measure. He used the good measure for his own cover. As a bonus, it afforded a cell phone signal.

"Could be the same outfit, but they brought a bigger trailer," Del reported. "Looks like twenty head. They've got good dogs. I'll give 'em that."

They'd brought in two dogs this time. Del was pretty sure the one they'd had with them last time around was the younger of the two. The older dog would be the one in the lead, the one getting right after those bovine back legs without making a fuss. The younger one was doing more barking than you'd want, but you still shouldn't go swatting him the way the numbskull with a quirt was doing.

Use the quirt on the cattle, you idiot. The dog is your partner.

"You're always judging rustlers by their dogs."

"I judge them by the way they treat their dogs. A good rustler takes care of his dog." If he could get his hands on that quirt right now, he knew what he'd do with it. "I'm bettin' Benson set Schrock up."

"Is he there?"

"He got out ahead of me, but it looks like his pickup is here."

"Why didn't you go with him?"

"Wasn't invited. Next time."

"You don't have a lot of time."

"When have I failed to deliver? Hell, by now I know what I'm doing, and *you* know that."

He felt as though he was watching a very long snake loop its body around its prey and haul it in, but it wasn't the body he was tasked with finding. It was the head. He had a role to play, and the reason he'd never failed was that he omitted nothing. He played his part, delivered his lines precisely.

But now there was Lila.

Except she was gone when he got back to the Short Straw Activity Center.

"Darlene took her home," Carl told him "Had to. She was looking for a ride, and she wasn't about to wait around." He clapped his hand on Del's back and peered up at him with eyes several beers' worth of serious. "Not a great start if you're trying to court the boss's daughter, my friend. And make no mistake about who's the boss of the Flynn Ranch. Brad Benson talks big, but he don't know a road apple from a cow pie." He glanced toward the door and his tone tempered. "Dar's back."

"What's wrong with you men?" she demanded.

"Us men? Don't lump me in with those bastards, honey."

She poked Del in the chest with a sharp red fingernail. "Barely get that woman to hop on the party boat, and then you leave her high and dry."

"I left her with you," he reminded her.

"And I took her home, which is where you'll find her if you've got a sincere apology on you somewhere."

"I wasn't gone *that* long."

"Long enough."

The bunkhouse was empty. Del expected a tail-wagging welcome, and the stillness was a disturbing disappointment. He was looking for rustlers. He didn't need to be complicating his assignment by looking for company. Even more disturbing was the too-tempting thought of finding the pup hanging out with more company he longed to keep. It was okay to enjoy their company, but he didn't need to be wanting it the way he did. Not a good sign for a committed loner.

But Asap had taken up residence with him, and a young roommate couldn't be allowed to go missing. And Lila deserved an apology.

The pup greeted him at the bottom of the porch steps. "Good boy." He didn't mind going down on one knee for a guy who didn't care where he'd been or what he'd done. He didn't much like feeling guilty. Guilt had been dogging him too damn long.

Lila's voice floated forth from the shadows. "He wouldn't come out of the bunkhouse at first."

He looked up, and there she was, standing at the top of the steps, still wearing that pretty blue dress. She descended on bare feet, sat down, tugged at her skirt so that it draped way down over her knees. Seated, she was forced to look up. He didn't want that. He took a seat beside her.

"I'm sorry, Lila. I didn't expect to get held up that long."

"You got held up?" She tipped her head sideways. He couldn't see light in her eyes, but there was a hint of it in her tone. "Was it a gang, or just one masked man?"

"What do you consider a gang?"

"I don't give much thought to gangs, not way out here. But I have to consider that you might be wearing a mask." She reached out and touched his cheek. "A very attractive mask, but still…"

"I'm really sorry. I got back as soon as I could."

"It doesn't matter." She took her hand away, but the warmth of her touch lingered. "I'd been there long enough. I'm not much of a party girl."

"Yeah, me, neither." They looked at each other. He tried out a sheepish smile, but she wasn't buying it. "I wanted to take you out, and Short Straw doesn't offer many options."

"No excuses?"

"Excuses only weaken the apology."

"Explanation?"

"You said it didn't matter."

"That's right, I did." She stacked her hands on her knees and rested her chin on them. "And it doesn't. It's done."

He scratched Asap's ears, then between his shoulders, the base of his spine, ruffling fur until the dog was ready to turn cartwheels for him. His dad had often told him that you could tell a lot about a man by a dog's first impression of him. *An animal doesn't care what you're wearing.* Lila was right about the mask, but it didn't bother Asap. And that was worth hanging on to.

"I have some land, too." Which had nothing to do with anything except that it was personal. It was a piece of him, a peace offering. "Along the Grand River, up by Mobridge. It's on the reservation. My dad left it to me. It's real pretty there, especially this time of year."

"You said your father was a rancher?"

"Cows and horses." He stretched one leg to a lower step and braced his forearm across the other knee, leaving a niche for Asap. "It wasn't a big operation, but the calf check paid the bills with a little left over, and the horses… Paints… Dad was known for his Paints. He didn't worry about registering them or anything like that. A Dan Fox Paint was worth more for how he was put together and what he could do than for any list of names on a piece of paper." He rubbed his thumb over the pup's soft ear. "That's what kept him going after my mother died."

"How old were you when she died?"

"I was five. Car accident. My father was driving." He gave that bit of information its due. A quiet moment. And then he launched into a torrent of detail. "Bad weather, bad roads, bad visibility, bad tires, all kinds of bad luck coming together in an instant. You can change a lot of things in life, but death ain't one of them."

"I know that. I do." A piece of her, a piece of him, something in common. No explanation could match that. "What happened to your father?"

"He put it behind him. The accident, not my mother's death. He never talked about any of it—it happened, she was gone, no use looking back—but he never stopped missing her. We were real tight, my dad and me. We didn't need anyone else. Oh, my aunts helped out, but mostly it was just us. We had a nice little calf crop every year, raised Paints, sold some beautiful saddle horses." He turned his head toward her. "I can put a real nice handle on a horse if you have a need. Do it for you in my spare time, just for the pleasure."

"I might take you up on that offer. But, of course, I'd pay for—"

"I said for the pleasure. And for you." He smiled. "Actions speak louder than explanations."

"You don't owe me anything, Del."

He turned his attention to the sky full of stars. "I learned a lot from my father. Pick yourself up. Cowboys don't cry. Put the past behind you. Pretty soon you've stacked up this big wall behind you, so there's no turning back. And that's good, as long as you can move day to day. As long as you can find some kind of a way ahead.

"We lost the cattle first. We had a bad winter— everyone lost some cattle—and then a bunch got stolen. Never recovered. When my father started talking about selling broodmares, I told him I didn't need to be going to college, I could hire out. Hell, I was a pretty good bronc rider, good enough to bring in some extra cash. But I was seventeen, and things weren't falling into place fast enough to suit me. I was making new friends, trying a few new things. Got arrested a couple of times."

He could feel her stiffen up a bit, and he held his

breath. She deserved a chance to ask the smart question. *For what?* And then he'd have to lie.

He was good at lying. It was all in a day's work, and he was good at his job. But he was telling her about his father, and it was all true so far. He didn't have a good lie on the tip of his tongue the way he always did when he was working a case.

But being with this woman didn't feel like part of the job. It should have, but it didn't. He wanted to pour everything out to her right here and now and see if she'd still be sitting beside him when he was done. He wanted to, but he didn't. And she kept quiet, too. Damn, but this was one patient woman.

"I gotta say, the court went pretty easy on me at first." He wasn't thinking to give her another opening, but his tongue thickened up for a moment.

And still she let him tell it his way.

"By then it was all about me. The cows were gone, horses were gone and my father took it hard, all of it. No turning back, no way forward. He was slipping away, and I didn't see it. You ask me, he died of a broken heart. Worn-out, maybe. Too many cracks. First heart attack laid him low. Within a few days the second one put him away."

"I'm sorry," she whispered.

"I can hear him laughing. 'What the hell are you talking about, a broken heart? Sounds pitiful.'" He chuckled as he turned to her. "He was a strong, quiet man. You'd've liked him, Lila. He'd've liked you."

"From what I'm hearing, I know I'm seeing him in you. I don't know about quiet," she excepted with a smile. "But strong. Caring."

He nodded. "He taught me better manners than I showed tonight."

"You're a pretty good dancer." She waited moment. "Now you can tell me I am, too."

"I don't know how it looked from the outside, but it sure felt sweet on the inside." Smiling, he took her face in his hands. "We were good together."

He kissed her hungrily, and he wanted so much more than the forgiving kiss she returned. She'd withdrawn from him some, but not all the way. She could have taken everything back, and he would have understood. But he wouldn't have given up, not the way he was feeling about her now. And she was willing to give him what she could, even though she didn't understand.

"You have to take a step back sometimes," he whispered across her lips. "Catch your breath."

Chapter Six

Lila's invitation for supper had been left open. Del kept thinking she would surprise him, but he didn't see her at all the following day. His day off. Hers, too. Not that he was keeping track, but if she'd wanted to spend time with him, he'd been handy. Proximity-wise. Now he decided to *get* handy, project-wise. Not that he had anything to prove on that score, but he liked to keep busy.

He went to the library. The librarian wasn't there, but he wasn't looking for her, and he was carrying a measuring tape to prove it. He had to borrow pencil and paper—maybe he wasn't *totally* prepared—but he ended up with his head in his plan. He and Asap took the long way back to the bunkhouse. The gardener wasn't in the garden. The teacher wasn't on the playground. Not that he needed a glimpse of her, or a word, or even a wave. The long way around was more scenic than the gravel driveway, that was all.

Well, that and it was filled with images of Lila.

By midnight he'd cut and sanded pieces for three bookcases. Frank had offered to help when he'd loaned him the tools, and Del had sensed some disappointment when he'd turned the old man down, but he made up for it by partnering with him in the hay fields early the next morning. Frank needed a hand, and Del hadn't been exaggerating when he'd declared himself to be a good one. He enjoyed the work. It reminded him of the years he'd had with his father. He hadn't been smart enough to value them at the time, but he valued his memories.

At midday he and Frank headed to the house for dinner. Del knew Lila wouldn't be there—didn't know why he even let the thought enter his mind—but he caught himself trying to think up reasons to call her, settled on "Would you mind taking Asap out?"

No answer.

Of course not. She had a life.

So did he, for crying out loud. He could damn sure take the time to take out his own dog.

His own dog. There. That was all he needed. A

guy had a life if he had a job, a good pickup and his own dog.

"You left early this morning, Brad," June was saying. The sound of her voice prompted Del to look down at his plate and notice—halfway through the meal—that he was eating chicken and rice. Not much taste to it. "Did you take Lila to do her shopping?"

"She didn't say nothin' about shopping. If she needs a ride, she'll let me know." Brad reached for the salt. "Won't she, Del? Del got her to go to the VFW dance. You believe that?"

"*Del* did?" June frowned at Brad, and then turned a look of wide-eyed wonder on Del.

"It was Brad's suggestion," Del said. Getting his head back into the game. He had a life, he had a job and Brad was his mark. "He was a little worried about her after we found the dog."

"Yeah, she took it pretty hard," Brad said. As if he would know.

"She introduced me around," Del said. "We had a good time."

"So what did *you* do this morning?" June asked her son.

"What did I do so far today?" Brad tapped his chin. "Well, let's see. I took a turn around the north pasture. We're still down six steers—they haven't wandered back—but otherwise the numbers add up.

More than you can say for Carl Schrock. Rustlers got to him next."

"Worse than coyotes," Frank grumbled. "They wait till the price goes up some, and then they swoop in, hit us from all directions. By the time the law draws a bead on them, they're gone. At least the coyotes belong here. They're *our* coyotes."

"A thief is a thief, Dad."

"Or a hunter," Del said quietly over a forkful of rice.

"Right." Frank poked his food around with his fork. "Coyotes have to hunt to eat. Otherwise they're just dogs. How many head did Schrock lose?"

"Twenty." Brad swallowed hard, glanced at Del and then settled back into himself with a shrug. "Or thereabouts. That's what I heard. He figured it happened while he was at the dance last night."

"Twenty head?" Frank glanced up from his plate. "He tallied up his losses that quick? Must've gotten out there and taken a count right away."

"I don't know for sure. That's just what people were saying today." Brad tried a change of subject on his mother. "Did a little shopping myself this morning. I needed to pick up a few things at the Co-Op, ran into the usual coffee crew. Fenton, Creitzer, that whole bunch."

"That whole bunch is my *old* bunch." Frank chuckled. "Bunch of semis, like me. Semiretired but still fully equipped."

"You're not their age, Frank." June raised the coffeepot in Del's direction.

He shook his head, doubled up with a no-more gesture, but thanked her with a smile. June's coffee was tolerable in small doses if you liked it strong enough to make a spoon stand up straight in the middle of your cup. Who knew what a potion like that could do to an old man's equipment?

"George Fenton wasn't too far ahead of me in school," Frank was saying. "Believe me, boys, it's beer with your buddies at Bucky's one day, coffee with the old coots at the Co-Op the next."

Del glanced up and favored Frank's joke with a chuckle, but in his mind one old man was gradually morphing into *the* old man, the one who was supposed to be too tough to die.

But he wasn't. And Frank reminded him of his own father.

"A friendly guy like me can handle both the same day," Brad said. "Tell you what, Del, you make hay while the sun shines this afternoon, and when it goes down tonight I'll buy you a beer. You'll be thirsty, and you won't want to stay that way, my friend."

"You're on."

The table talk went on around him, but Del had withdrawn. Brad was on for more than a beer. He was in for the kind of trouble Del had known firsthand, the kind sure to dump distress on an old man's doorstep. And Del was about to help bring it on. Oh, sure, he knew Brad was the one about to land in some very deep, very hot water, but the ripples would hit the whole Flynn family.

And he also knew he was letting himself get too close.

Sundown did nothing to relieve the day's heat. Beer with the boys at Bucky's wasn't exactly Del's idea of a fun night, but he didn't keep time by the clock. Not in his line of work. Hanging out, nursing a beer, losing a game of pool he could easily win—sounded like a dream job. But closing the deal could be a killer.

"Two in the corner."

Click. Blue went down.

Del nodded. "You're good, Brad."

"Practice." Grinning, Brad chalked his cue. "Nobody wants to take me on anymore."

"It's like watching a game on TV. You start getting the itch to play, but your turn never comes."

"I don't mind stepping aside. You wanna break next time?"

"Yeah, it's time I caught a break. But you don't need to step aside." Del glanced over at the bar. Three guys at the far end were crooning along with Garth Brooks about friends in low places. And Brad missed his shot. "That was a nice piece of work out at Schrock's place. Bigger trailer, bigger haul."

Brad frowned as he lowered his cue. "You were there?"

"You and me, boss." Del motioned for the chalk. "We were both there."

"But you were with Lila."

"Yeah, she's not too happy with me for leaving her. She caught a ride with Darlene."

"Schrock?"

"Yeah, Darlene Schrock. The irony, huh?" Del blew chalk off the tip of his cue. "Look, I'm not here to make trouble. I want in."

"In what?"

Del offered a knowing smile.

"If you were there, you might've noticed I wasn't really involved."

"You're involved, my friend. A bit player, maybe, but your ass is branded." Del studied the table. "You're the inside man. They tell you what they're looking for and you supply all the information they need. You come up with the time and the place, best ways in and out, and you sell out your neighbors, maybe even your family. That's the way it works." He sighted along his cue. "Three in the side." The red ball rolled into the hole. "You don't have to say anything, Brad. I've got eyes. I've been out of the game for a while, but I know the drill. Got into it probably the same way you did. I wanted something for myself."

"Everybody loses a few head every year. One way or another, it's part of the business."

"Sure it is." Del described his next shot and then banked the purple ball into the corner. "Tax write-off, right? That's what you tell yourself. It won't hurt the Double F. Won't hurt the Schrocks. Some guys carry insurance, some don't, but you tell yourself they'll all recover. Some sooner than others, but you figure they'll come out okay in the end. Anybody who goes under from the loss of just a few head was already teetering on the edge. You did him a favor by nudging him over. He's better off working for wages."

"Look, I gave you a job. You want more money? I'll come up with more money." Brad stepped closer. "I don't know how to get you in. Like you said, I'm just a bit player."

Del smiled. "It's kind of a rush, isn't it?"

"Watching some guys load up a few cows?"

"It's like winning at poker on a bluff. You rake in the pot, now you're really a player. Hell, Benson, you're a cattle rustler." Del shrugged. "Hey, there's good money in it. But you gotta learn a few more skills, work your way up."

"I'm not goin' anywhere. When they move on, I'll have something to tide me over."

"So will I." Another shot, another hit. Del kept talking while he lined up his next move. "When you get your next call, tell them your hired hand's interested in trying out for a role. Tell them he's had some experience."

"Okay, I'll give it a shot."

"Thanks." Del racked his cue. "Maybe I'll see you in the morning."

"Where are you going?"

"I'm a workin' man, Brad. Gotta get to bed on time if I'm gonna keep up with Frank tomorrow." He chuckled. "That man is hell on tractor wheels."

The lights were on in the schoolhouse, and the dog was missing from the bunkhouse. The woman had left him a trail of bread crumbs, which he was sorely tempted to ignore.

No, he wasn't. Not sorely. Not even slightly. There wasn't a cell in Del's body willing to turn away from the light in those schoolhouse windows. Gravel crunched beneath his boot heels and crickets cheered him on as he topped the rise in the driveway that curved through the grass. A shadow flitted past the window, which then went dark. He stopped in his tracks. The door opened and shut, and two shadows approached—the small one loped along, the tall one glided and neither spoke to him.

Asap reached him first. He gave the pup's floppy ears a tousle. Lila's footsteps slowed, and Del's heart pounded so hard he was sure she could hear it. He reached for her, and she leaned into him, slid her arms around him and lifted her face to his. Their kiss was all consuming. Her throat vibrated with a needy moan, his chest with a hungry groan. He plunged his tongue past her lips, held her close, their bodies fully flush. She welcomed him entirely, moved with him mouth to mouth and hip to hip, and every fiber of his being, every filament of hers, was infused into the kiss they made together.

In the breathless moment that followed, they agreed without saying a word. She took his hand, and he knew where they were going. Her place. The room filled with Lila, where she felt secure enough to let him come to know her. And know her he would.

There was a storm coming. Lila had felt it, had known even before darkness had fallen, and now she squeezed his hand and lifted her face to the first dollops of rain. It would be hard and heavy, but it would relieve the heat and clear the air.

She'd been ready for this—for him—for hours. Days. Maybe her whole life. She laughed, and she would have quickened her steps, but she'd left her flip-flops in the schoolhouse. Del tugged on her hand, whirled her around the way he had when they'd danced together, but this time he swept her into his arms and somehow kissed her and carried her and climbed the front steps without the slightest hesitation. Later she would relive this night, and this part would have her smiling right from the start, but right now her body was eager to move past it.

He let her legs slip, her body slide over his, her feet find purchase on the porch as he kissed her from a different angle. She met his kiss with her own and happily gave it back. She grabbed the screen door, threw it open and pulled him in after her. He followed her up the stairs. It wasn't until they reached the top that the pup came bounding after them. Another time she would have laughed, but not now. She could hardly breathe, but somehow her chest swelled and her heart fluttered. Deep down she shivered and quivered and burned all at once.

She hadn't made her bed that morning, but she lacked the presence of mind to care as she fumbled with the snap on her jeans.

He pushed her hands aside and whispered, "This is for me to do."

He kissed her again, and before she could do more than nibble his generous lips he was sliding her jeans over her hips, dropping to his knees and one at a time lifting her feet clear of the rain-damp denim. He kissed her belly, then licked and play-bit while his thumbs slowly dragged her cotton panties below her hip bones. She plunged her fingers into his thick hair and pressed her nails into his scalp. She was wet now, and the rain could not be blamed.

He feathered his lips lower, dispatched her panties and then rubbed his chin back and forth, ruffling her tight curls as he gently slid his thumbs into the folds of her groin. So close. So tantalizingly close. She tried not to look, but she had to, and there were his smiling eyes, waiting for some signal. She answered yes with a slight shift of her hips, and he teased with a flickering tongue until her breath quivered and she shivered deep down.

She bit her bottom lip. Every part of her wanted to be touched. It almost hurt to stretch her fingers and let go of his hair, almost pained her to draw breath and feel her bra abrade her nipples, almost killed her when his hands left her even momentarily. He stood, took hold of her bottom, lifted her and pulled her to him, oh, yes, and rocked against her and kissed her, plunged his tongue in and out until she caught it, and yes, she sucked it as she tugged at his zipper, and yes, it gave way.

Her T-shirt came off, her bra slid away and she was on the bed, unsure of how she got there, unsure of anything except that she ached, everything tingled and ached, and when he touched her the tingling stung sweetly and the aching throbbed terribly. His incorrigible mouth made her nipples so tight they threatened to explode, while his maddeningly slow, deft touch between her legs, into her secret folds, around her most sensitive flesh, had her palpitating with such wild abandon that her whole body gave in to wave after wave of pure pleasure.

She couldn't stop, and he wouldn't let her. He

drew her hand to his penis and whispered, "Touch me, Lila. That's all I need."

But *she* needed more. Much more. He gasped when she drew him inside her, lifted her hips and held him hard, then rocked him as only a woman's body could rock a man. She gave him no quarter, no option but to answer with the matching motion of his own hips. He stroked inside her until she called his name and shuddered blissfully, and he, marvelous man, swiftly withdrew and flooded her belly.

And for the first time that night she was aware of rain on the roof, wind rattling the trees and thunder rumbling in the night.

They held each other for a time neither measured, resting, caressing, listening to the rain, admiring each other's body when a flash of lightning filled the room.

"I was afraid you wouldn't come tonight," she said finally. Her voice sounded deeper than she remembered it from…when? An hour, a day, a lifetime ago?

"Didn't want to come too soon." He chuckled. "You knew that was coming."

"I should have." Lightning flashed, thunder rolled and a wet nose nudged her hand. "Ace! Have you been here all along? You bad boy." She wasn't sure why. It was Bingo who'd always seemed human, and Asap wasn't Bingo.

"That would be me. I'm the bad boy." He held

up a hand. "No dogs on the bed, Asap. We've been over that." He curled his arm around Lila. "Only the alpha gets on the bed." He turned back to Lila. "And yes, you should've known I'd come."

"Why did it take you so long?"

"I was afraid you'd turn me away."

"I planned to." She snuggled against his shoulder. "I took my horse out for a long ride yesterday, visited a friend, a man I know you'd like. His daughter was my best friend growing up. I was gone all day."

"Mmm-hmm."

"You noticed?"

"Maybe."

"Well, I wasn't angry. It wasn't that important, our little date. But if you'd shown up last night, it was going to be...different."

"Because?"

"Because, because."

Senseless answer. She wanted to take it back before he took advantage with a quip or a quote, something smart. She had no answers, not even for herself.

But he kissed her temple—tenderness for a tender place—and whispered, "How did you know I was coming up the driveway?"

"Ace let me know you were out there."

She'd turned off the light, looked through the window and then she'd been on her way out the door, because he'd been there. Heart pounding, pulse racing, his name her only clear thought, she'd slid through the dark to be with him.

"I knew you were gone yesterday," he told her. "Last night I started making bookcases."

"You did?"

"They're just pieces so far. You can still make changes on anything but the size."

"Where? There's nothing…"

"Down in the shop. Frank let me use his tools." She felt him smile against her temple. "I told him I'd always wanted to build a library. He asked if I needed help, but I told him I wasn't sure exactly what I was going to do. I think he knew what I meant. I hope he did. I start with a plan, and then it's trial and error until I find the finished product. It's hard to work with somebody else when you're flying by the seat of your pants."

He was making bookcases. *For her.*

"And I borrowed a couple of books from the library. How long do I get to keep them out?"

"As long as you need to. What are you reading?"

"A Western. I've read it before, so I'll get through it quick."

"A comfort read, huh?"

"An old friend." His lips stirred her hair as he spoke.

The rain pattered steadily, and the wind still blew, but the thunder's rumble was distant now. Maybe the storm was going away.

"Tell me about your friend and his daughter."

"Crystal Chasing Elk and I started the day care business together after I came back from Minnesota."

He stilled for a moment, midbreath. "Chasing Elk?"

"Uh-huh. Her father is Stan. You know him?"

"No."

"I'll have to introduce you. Anyway, I didn't come back right away after the accident, but when I couldn't get myself together enough to make any sense of what I was doing, I left school. This house had been empty for years, so I asked Crystal to move in with me, and we fixed the place up. The day care was her idea. She'd been thinking about it, had some people interested, just didn't have a place. This was perfect.

"She was the driving force behind it, she… Well, she did all the driving. We had more kids then. I didn't know she was sick. I mean, I knew she was diabetic, but I didn't know she was having problems with her kidneys." She sighed. It was hard to admit she hadn't known how sick Crystal had been. If she had just pulled her head out of her butt sooner… "I couldn't even give her one of mine. We weren't compatible. We were *so* compatible, like sisters, in every other way. But my extra kidney was useless to her."

She laid her hand on Del's sturdy chest and felt

the beat his heart. "I wish you could have met her. You really would have liked her."

"I could have been compatible."

"If you were, would you have…?"

"No question." He covered her hand with his. "Yeah, that's something I would do. That would be easy." He gave a dry chuckle. "Whether I liked her or not. I mean, they give you some kind of drugs, you go to sleep, you wake up, maybe there's a little scar, but otherwise you don't miss a kidney."

"You could." She kissed his shoulder. "If you're down to one."

"Last time I checked my birth certificate, there were no guarantees on parts, and the cost of repairs has gone through the roof. But if you can find a used kidney…" She thumped him. *"Oof!"*

His sense of humor was so much like Crystal's, it might have been a transplant. "She would have liked you. After you blew me off at the dance—"

"I what?"

"—she would've said, 'I told you, never trust a cowboy.' But those bookcases…"

"You don't have them yet."

"But I will. You strike me as a man who finishes what he starts. Anyway, you did. You blew me off. But when I saw you outside tonight, I knew how I felt. I know you."

"Feeling and knowing are two different things."

"True. So tell me what else I should know."

"I could tell you anything right now, couldn't I? Think about that, Lila. Think about what your friend would tell you, what she'd tell you now."

"Crystal didn't—"

"You know, you shouldn't be saying her name, since she's dead. Lakota, right?"

"What difference does that make?"

"Speaking their names can hold them here," he said solemnly, and then he made a funny sound in his throat, like an uneasy chuckle. "That's what they say anyway. I don't know if I believe it, but just in case… It's not fair to hold them here, you know? Let them go free." He paused. "Does that sound crazy?"

"No." In fact, she liked the idea. She could picture her friend's release, an ethereal spirit with smiling eyes and no need for a name.

"Superstitious?"

"Not if it's what you believe."

"My dad believed it. I respect him. Always did. I don't know what I…" He drew a deep breath and sighed. "Lila, I had to go with Brad. I saw him leave, and I had to go right away. There was no time to discuss, explain, none of that."

"He really isn't your boss, Del."

"I know. Your dad writes the checks." He nuzzled her hair. "I like Frank. He's a good man."

"He's henpecked."

Del chuckled. "Must be why my dad didn't go for the second wife. You notice I don't say his name.

That's the part that ties a spirit down. That earth name."

"Would you like to meet Crystal's father?" He groaned. "I say her name a lot. I'm not Lakota."

"Like I said, I'm not too traditional. I just…" He shook his head. "Yeah, I'd like to meet Stan Chasing Elk."

"I'll take you there. We'll ride. Whenever you have time."

"I'll make time." He reached for the sheet, pulled it across their no-guarantees bodies, and they cuddled. "Man, that wind sounds strong."

"We should move to the basement," she said. Again he groaned. "I have a storm shelter down there. Food, water, blankets, flashlights. All the necessities. We put it together mostly for the kids." He didn't move. "There's a sofa."

"I like it here." He kissed her breast all around her nipple, which he then licked. "I'm blowing you off," he said, and he blew softly, steadily.

A rumble of thunder. A howling wind. Lightning split the darkness in two. Lila stiffened. Asap whined.

Del sighed. "Okay, honey, take me down."

He woke up during the night, confused at first about where he was. It was pitch-dark, and his ass was cold. But his arms were full of warm, soft, musk-scented woman, and he was stiff all over. But mostly where it counted.

She stirred in his arms, and he grew harder. He was going to have to do something about that. Either get up or something else. Something better.

"Is it morning?" she asked.

"Feels like it."

"Do you think that was a tornado that came through?"

He smiled against the dark. "I got hit pretty hard by something. How about you?"

"Want some breakfast?"

The chance for something better was going to slip away if he didn't make something happen fast. "After we take a shower."

"You shower while I make breakfast." She started to climb over him.

He stopped her midway, took a thigh in each hand and made her straddle him. "One false move and you're ready for the grill, darlin'. Chick on a stick."

"You really are a bad boy."

"Fire or water? Your call. You take a shower with me. I'll fix breakfast for you."

"Save the fire for February. What do you want to fix? I might not have everything you need."

"You do, my pretty." He bounced her once and unleashed a mock evil laugh. "Everything."

She ran for the stairs wrapped in a blanket. Del

brought up the rear, and his was buck naked. He tried to snatch the blanket, but she shrieked and then tripped on the damn thing, and he felt like a real dog. An indignant yip from the real dog at the foot of the stairs made him slow down. He might have made up for his bone-headed play by scooping Lila up and carrying her the rest of the way, but the stairs were narrow, and falling down them bare assed would have spoiled what was left of the mood.

Instead he steadied himself on the railing with one hand and slid the other around her waist. "You okay? I'm…" Oh, God, she was shaking. "Lila? Where does it—"

"Let go of me, please."

He stepped down slowly and dropped his arm to his side.

The blanket dropped over his head, and he heard feet pounding up the steps.

"Damn it, woman!"

By the time he reached the bathroom she was stepping into the shower, laughing like a little girl. He barreled in after her, backed her under the water and kissed her until they both nearly drowned.

"You scared me, you know that?" he said.

Of course she did. She was still giggling, hair plastered to her head, eyelashes all spiky and her eyes sparkling like Christmas morning. She looked so perfect that he was almost afraid to touch her.

He grabbed a bar of wet soap and started rolling it between his hands.

"You were chasing me."

"Did you get hurt?" He set the soap aside and sudsed up her shoulders. "It was the damn blanket that tripped you up, not me. What were you trying to cover up?"

"I was running up the stairs. And I was jiggling!"

"So you covered up?" He laughed. "I was jiggling, too."

She spared his erection a quick glance. "That's basically one, well…" She cupped her breasts. "I have two of these, and they're boneless." She reached around back. "And this jiggles, too, and I'm just not the jiggling type."

"You're a funny girl." He drew her hand away from her body and claimed it for himself, tucking it between his legs. "I don't think too much about how things look." He slid his hands up her torso. It was his turn to cup her breasts. He smiled as he thumbed her nipples. "Boneless and beautiful. Tasty, too."

She closed her eyes. "Don't stop." Her hand intensified her persuasiveness.

He rested his forehead on hers, and they brought each other to heavenly heights without giving another thought to jiggling.

Lila stood looking out the bathroom window, a white towel wrapped around her chest. Del ruf-

fled his hair with the towel he'd used to dry himself. "Something wrong?" he asked as he tucked it
around his waist.

"The storm. There's a lot of debris, looks like
a lot of damage. The fence, the play yard, the
garden…" She leaned to one side. "The barn looks
okay, but I can't see it all, can't see the corral. The
horses…"

"They'll be in the barn. I'll go."

"And the schoolhouse. I can't tell from here."

She turned to him, and she looked scared. Scared
for her animals, her fruits and flowers, her sanc-
tuary. And that schoolhouse, with its memories,
mysteries, history… It meant more to her than
the typical bygone-era castoff that thrifty farmers
bought for a song and parked behind the barn for
just in case. Lila was more builder than collector,
and she built dreams. She was bringing new life to
that old schoolhouse.

And whatever was out there now, whatever the
condition, he wanted to see it before she did.

"Wait for me, Del."

"I'm gonna grab my pants and take the dog out
real quick." He looked back and nodded. "Let me
go first."

Chapter Seven

Eager to run off the night's jitters, the two horses charged past Del and into their little pasture as soon as he opened the gate. Other than a little roof damage, the outbuildings below the hill had fared well. It was a relief to report good news when Lila met him at the kitchen door. And it was a pleasure to smell coffee and bacon.

"No injuries to the livestock, all the buildings are still standing and my job is secure."

"The new house came through fine. I called. Dad said the wind lifted a few shingles, but nothing major." She handed him a cup of hot coffee. "Your job is to keep him off the roof."

"I'm the hired hand. My job is to be handy."

"I didn't hire you." She gestured toward the kitchen table with the gray Formica top and stainless-steel trim. He'd grown up with one almost like it. "But I'll feed you, even though I *did* share the shower." She set a plate in front of him. "I hope you like your eggs scrambled. I know every inch of your body, but I have no idea what you like for breakfast."

"Anything jiggly and boneless." He flashed her a wink, and he picked up his fork. "I'll work it out with Frank and fix what needs fixing. It's mostly the yard. There's a little water damage inside the schoolhouse. Lots of shingling to be done, but I'm good with heights."

"I want to go over and check on Stan. I called, but there was no answer." She joined Del at the table. "I turned on the news. No tornado touchdown was reported, but some places lost power. Do you have time to give me a ride? It's not far. It won't take long."

"Over to Stan Chasing Elk's? Sure. The man's had his share of troubles lately."

She gave him a funny look. "I thought you didn't know him."

"I know *of* him. Last night you told me he's your friend, your friend's father. That's all the endorsement I need."

"What do you mean?" She frowned. "Did Brad

accuse him of something? Because if he did…" She shook her head. "We don't need Twitter around here. We've got Brad Benson. He has a habit of repeating rumor as fact."

"I can generally tell the difference."

She was quiet for a moment. Then defensive, as though someone had accused *her* of something. "There is no way he stole any cattle."

He lifted one shoulder. *Back on the job*. "When there's a lot of talk, you reach for the salt."

"It's beer talk. Bar stool babble." She pushed her chair back from the table. "I need a ride over there. You can just drop me off."

"You said I could meet your friend. I can do that now if I can talk your dad into staying off the roof until I get back."

Stanley Chasing Elk lived a small house flanked by a cottonwood and chokecherry shelter that stood beside a creek fed by runoff from a cluster of rolling hills a few miles away. His pole barn was twice as big as his house, and he seemed to be running more chickens than cows these days.

He was standing on the front step when they drove into the yard. He was a tall man who cut an imposing figure in his crisp plaid Western shirt, cowboy boots and the graying braids gracing his shoulders. He would have seen their pickup turn off the blacktop highway onto his rutted approach from more than a mile away. He lived alone now, and his once-thriving ranch saw few visitors.

Lila greeted him with the embrace of a daughter for her father. "I tried to call, but you didn't answer. I was worried."

"The storm passed by me. Thunderbird decided I'd had enough trouble lately."

Lila slid Del a glance. He was staring at the ground, waiting his turn.

"Who's this you brought?" Stan asked.

Del stepped up quickly and introduced himself with a traditional slight-grip handshake.

"Fox? Some Foxes up by New Town." Stan turned to Lila. "I just made coffee." She nodded and went into the house, pleased to be treated like a daughter.

She knew the Chasing Elk kitchen as well as her own. When she returned with coffee and cups, she knew that little had been said in her absence. Stan stood with his arms folded across his chest, Del with thumbs hooked into the front pockets of his jeans, both staring past Stan's empty corral, seemingly watching cloud shadows slide across the waving prairie grass. They were either waiting for her or the coffee to get the visit started.

Del took two cups from her and handed one to Stan, who nodded toward the redwood picnic table beneath the rustic round "shade" made of stripped poles and thatched with cottonwood branches.

"But you're not from Fort Berthold," Stan said, as though he had last spoken only thirty seconds ago.

"Hell no. I'm Lakota. My father was from Standing Rock." Del waited until Lila and Stan were seated across from each other before he took his place beside her on the bench.

"Don't know any Foxes up there. But I don't know everybody." Stan sipped his coffee. "Small world, Indian country. You get to be as old as I am, you think you know everybody. But you don't." He lifted his chin and gave Del a considering look. "I can tell you're from Standing Rock. You've got that look, like you've been out in the sun too long."

"You talk like my father." Del nodded. "I haven't been this far south that much. I thought you'd be a lot shorter."

Stan nodded back at Del, then turned to Lila with a broad grin. "Good man. Where did you find him, my girl?"

Del couldn't help feeling warmed by the old man's praise, but he kept his face impassive.

"Brad hired him. But you mustn't hold that against him, Stan. He's making me bookcases."

"For the library? Good man, good man. Be sure the children can reach their books on their own. We want them to find books without being told."

"Stan built the children's shelves for us. That was back when we were fixing it up just for day care.

It was all about making everything child-size, and I wanted it all 'One Little, Two Little, Three Little Indians' at first, but I was told to get real." She flashed a smile Stan's way.

"Not by me. They're little Indian kids. There's nothing wrong with counting them."

"She'd hated the song ever since she was in preschool because it was only about boys. 'What about us girls?' she said."

"That was my daughter," Stan said to Del. "Always wanted everything just so. Just like this one." He nodded at Lila. "They were like sisters. They'd butt heads over something one day, go off not speaking, next day they've got it figured out."

"So we decided on the colors of the four directions, and each color was a station for stories and singing and snacking and sleeping."

"My kind of school," Del said.

"We'd barely gotten started," Lila said. "We had so many more ideas. She was a bundle of energy."

"She was that." Stan patted Lila's hand. "So are you. And I know it was hard on you when she died."

"Hard on *me*?" Lila put her other hand over the old man's. "I should have seen it coming. She was young and strong, and when she came back from her clinic appointments and I asked, 'How's it going?' and she said, 'Good,' that was all I wanted to hear. And then she was gone.

"I'm a wimp, Stan. I almost went back into the

shell that Crys—that your daughter pried me out of. If it wasn't for you…" She turned to Del. "It took me too long to reopen. I lost most of the kids."

"But then they came back, some of them," Stan said. "Isn't that so, my girl?"

"Yes, because you talked me up with the parents. They weren't sure I'd stick with the program on my own. They came for…" She glanced at Del. "I didn't know I wasn't supposed to be saying her name."

"You told her that?" Stan asked Del.

"Well, yeah." He shrugged. "Wasn't I supposed to?"

"It don't matter. The *wanagi* only hear *us*."

"My mistake." Del flashed Lila a sly wink. "Guess you don't count with the Lakota spirits."

"Really?"

He squeezed her shoulder. "Don't take it personal." And then he grinned at Stan, and they both chuckled.

"Is it true or not?" Lila insisted.

"It is until we find out different," Stan said.

"Which I'm not planning to do any time soon," Del added.

"You two must be related," Lila grumbled good-naturedly. "Indian humor. I never know how to react until you say *just kidding*."

"Did you say it?" Del asked Stan. "I know I didn't say it."

"Well, I know I'm not taking any chances," Lila

said. "I don't need to speak her name. I have much more to remember her by."

Stan patted her hand again. She offered a misty smile and then cleared her throat. "Dad lost some steers. He thinks they were stolen. Well, Brad thinks they were stolen, and Darrell Hartley—"

"Sheriff Hartley probably thinks I stole them. I had a visit from the tribal police."

Lila frowned. "They don't really think you stole them, do they?"

"They think maybe I know something about it." Stan wrapped his big, leathery hands around his cup. "I pastured tribal cattle until most of them disappeared a while back," he told Del. "They had all kinds of cops out here looking for some way to prove I was in on the disappearance, but they couldn't come up with anything.

"Lost some of my own cattle, too, so I'm not in the cattle business anymore. Sold all but twenty head when I lost my lease. They'll have to dig around in somebody else's backyard. Maybe that big shot from the college, that Klein."

"Didn't they fire him?" Lila asked.

"Yeah, because he bought a bunch of equipment for the ag program and took it to his own place."

"Did they get the equipment back?" Del asked.

Stan lifted one shoulder. "They got a tractor back that was five years older than the one he *borrowed*, a busted backhoe and I don't know what all else."

"There should've been paperwork on the equipment," Del said.

"Should've." Stan gave a humorless smile. "Turned out Professor Klein wasn't too good with paperwork. He could've *sworn* everything was in those files."

"Could've or did?" Del had heard stories like this before.

"All I know is he had a lawyer." Stan shook his head in disgust. "Tribal colleges get themselves into a bind over contracts like everyone else. The tribe had to pay him to be rid of him. Nobody paid me, but I'm not in prison, so that's something."

Lila laid her hand on the old man's plaid sleeve. "You were never charged with anything, Stan."

"Ninety-six head," Stan said angrily. "Somebody got away as slick as bear grease with ninety-six head."

"Looks like somebody's back for more," Del said.

"It wouldn't be the same outfit, would it? They wouldn't try hitting the same place again. That wouldn't be too smart." Stan scowled. "Course the tribe's cattle aren't in the same place." His face broke into a sly smile. "I hope it *is* the same damn bunch of thieves. Hell, they'll get caught this time for sure."

"How many head does the tribe have left?"

"I wouldn't know. None on my land. I check mine

pretty often, and I know what's here. I can count to twenty pretty easy."

"If you need anything…" Lila said quietly.

"Don't you start now. I've got all I need except something to do." The old man glanced at Del. "Maybe you'd let me help out with those book-cases."

"We got broken swings, busted fence and some water damage in the library. Plenty to do whenever you wanna jump in," Del said.

Stan looked at Lila. "I'm hearin' a lotta *we*. Who did you say this man's workin' for?"

Del smiled. "I'm like you, Stan. I like to keep busy."

On the way back to the Double F, Del waited for Lila to tell him what she needed first. The air in the little space they shared was filled with frustration, and she didn't know the half of it. But the half she knew was heavy enough.

She'd gotten herself mixed up with a man she didn't know much about, and what she did know couldn't be sitting too well with her. The old man she did know well was suspected of something she knew he couldn't have done. Maybe the problem she was sitting with was also the *man* she was sit-ting with. If she asked him straight-out, he had to be ready with a lie or some kind of half-truth— *same as a lie, Fox, be honest in your own head, at least*—and he didn't know if he could come up with anything right now.

What kind of help could he offer? What did she need?

"Do you still have a driver's license?" he asked finally.

"I do. It's handy for identification. I don't have a car, though."

"How about insurance?"

"I had good insurance. Everything was covered."

Ah, the accident. That wasn't where he'd been going with his questions, but he was more than willing to follow her lead.

"There was a child, wasn't there?"

She said nothing, and the moment drew out. It was up to her.

"Yes. A child."

"And it wasn't your fault." He was no therapist, but some things were obvious, and it couldn't hurt to say them. As long as it wasn't about him.

"It wasn't the little girl's fault. It wasn't her father's fault."

"Her father?"

"The poor guy. He tried to…" She drew a deep, unsteady breath. "I don't want to talk about this, Del. I've made my peace with it. At least I think I have. And every time I say that, I think, who am I to make peace? And then the dreams come back."

"Yeah, I know about dreams." Not like she did.

There were no children in his dreams. Everyone he'd ever hit had been a man who'd been begging Del to slam a fist into his gut. Those were the good dreams.

"I was driving, but I wasn't charged with anything. Officially, it was nobody's fault." Her voice dropped. He had to strain to catch every word. "It was bad. It doesn't matter how it came about. It's *what* came about that matters. Talking about it changes nothing."

"I know. I was just thinking, if you ever feel like you want to try driving again, maybe I could help you."

"I'm doing just fine. I know how to drive. I choose not to."

"Okay. What do you want me to hit first?"

"Hit?"

He smiled. "The fence? The swings? Maybe the schoolhouse roof in case we get more rain, but I'd have to get shingles."

"You don't work for me, Del."

"I'm gonna go down and talk to Frank. Meanwhile, you make a general plan."

Again she was quiet, and he thought he'd lost her. But then she perked up some, smiled wistfully. "I get to be the general?"

"How about the queen?" he offered. "I wouldn't make it as a soldier."

He was gone longer than he'd thought he would be. He and Frank checked the hay field and agreed that it was too wet to work it, but a full day of sun would make all the difference. Frank seemed happy with Del's concern for the damage at the home place and his assurance that he could fix it all, and Brad readily agreed to check cows after he picked up Del's list of building materials. Del exchanged a look with Frank. They both knew what Brad's idea of checking cows was. Kill a little time driving around in his pickup, come back for dinner and report that everything was looking good.

Lila had piled up some debris in front of the schoolhouse and the edge of the play yard, and she was working on the garden, tossing ruined plants into a wheelbarrow, muttering as she worked. "Damn storm." Golf ball–size green tomatoes rattled as they hit. "Damn badger. Damn rattler. Damn, damn—"

Del walked up to the wheelbarrow and offered her his gloves. "Either put these on or take a seat on the throne." She glowered at him, and he smiled. "I'm yours for the rest of the day." He snapped the gloves. "What's the plan?"

"I have gloves."

"And blisters."

"They're almost…" She turned her hands and they both saw the traces of blood mixed with dirt. "All right. You're right. I was just going to clear away some of it so I could see if there's anything left, and the more I cleared—"

"The more you cussed."

"Waste of breath, right?" She wiped her forehead with the back of her hand as she surveyed the jumbled garden. "There won't be many tomatoes."

"This should cheer you up. Brad's gonna go get us some shingles."

"Brad is?"

"And some woven wire. And some posts. Glass for the window. I'll have to take that sucker apart. Can you think of anything else? I'll add it to the order."

"And I have you for the day? How did you manage that?"

"Hey, your dear stepbrother just wants to help out."

"What*ever*."

"He knows they dodged a bullet down at the new house, and you caught one up here. Everybody pitches in." He grinned. "Don't look a gift horse in the mouth, woman."

"Is that what you are?"

"Could be." He reached for her hand. "After we clean you up again, is this where you want to start?"

"I want to save as much of the garden as I can. I'm going to put a raised bed over Bingo. I'll grow special things there, like herbs and healing plants." She took another wistful look. "I started a lot of this from seed. Even the tomatoes."

"Tell me what you want me to do," he said as they walked back to the house.

"Let's clean up the garden, then the schoolhouse and then the fence. Or the play yard. We'll need the..." She looked up at him and smiled. She seemed happy to have him. "Let's work together. I'll try not to cuss."

"Me, too."

Once he was satisfied that her hands were protected, they made short work of the garden cleanup. He claimed the rake and garden fork, and she was allowed to judge each plant's chances for recovery. He had her joking about the powers of royalty. But he was the one who kept coming up with ideas for improvements on top of repairs.

"Hey, how about putting rocks around these flower beds?" he asked as they rounded the corner of the house pushing a wheelbarrow full of discards toward the appropriate pile. "Nobody's gonna drive over rocks, and there's a whole pile of them behind the bunkhouse."

"I love that idea. I'll put it on my list."

"Put it on *my* list." He upended the wheelbarrow. "I'll have to replace that broken window out in the schoolhouse, but I should be able to use the old frame. I don't suppose you'd want to upgrade those windows? What do you do for heat in the winter?"

"In the library I burn wood and wear a coat. We were saving up to put in propane heat, but we didn't get that far, so I made it a library. I mean, we needed a library. The kids like to come in here until it gets too cold, and then we stay in the house a lot. If I get more kids…" She turned and appeared to be speaking to the schoolhouse when she asked, "How long are you going to stay?"

He couldn't give his usual answer. *Couldn't say.* "All I know is I get paid by the month."

"How long do you usually stay?"

"As long as the job lasts." He was glad to see some activity at the Double F gate. "Here comes our delivery truck." Briefly getting him off the hook.

A clacking noise below her bedroom window pulled Lila to the surface of sleep. It was still dark. The middle of the night, said the bright numbers on her bedside clock. She peeked outside and saw Del's pickup. He was standing in the bed, heaving huge rocks over the side.

"Hey." He dropped to the ground and shed his leather work gloves as she approached, harsh words dissolving on her tongue when she saw his beautiful face close up in the moonlight. "I couldn't sleep. Couldn't stop thinking about moving these rocks."

She smiled. "It's a lovely night for moving rocks."

"Great night for it."

"As hard as you worked today, you should be sleeping like a baby."

"How do babies sleep? Don't they wake up every

few hours?" He sat down on the pickup tailgate and beckoned her with a gesture. "I wake up sometimes and feel like the walls are closing in. I have to go outside and get some air."

"It's a wonder you were able to sleep down in the basement."

"I was with you." He reached for her and drew her between his knees. "I slept like a baby. Face between your breasts."

"Want to try that again? Upstairs this time."

"I do. Upstairs, downstairs, under the stairs, I'd sleep with you anywhere, darlin'. Right now…" He nodded toward a patch of once-tall coneflowers and bushy Shasta daisies, some lying low, some still standing. "Once I get started on something, I like to get it to the point where it starts to look like what I pictured. Then I know I'll finish it. Until then, I won't be able to sleep."

"I couldn't really sleep, either."

"Did I wake you up?" He chucked her chin. "Did you miss me?"

"I'm afraid I will. Who will I have to talk to besides four-year-olds and the wolf at the door?"

"Don't let him in, honey. He can't replace the Fox."

She boosted herself up to join him on the tailgate. He slipped his arm around her, and she put her head on his shoulder. She could get used to this. The sex was surprising and risky and amazing, but this quiet comfort… It surprised her almost as much. She had come by it without seeking it, like hunting for wild turnips and discovering a pasqueflower blooming out of season.

"The child I hit was only five," she told him. Unplanned, unrehearsed, the story simply rolled off her tongue into the cool night air. "It was winter. Dusk. She came shooting out of a driveway on a little blue plastic sled. It happened so fast. I heard a terrible scream. I didn't even know what I'd hit until I got out of the car. It was her father who screamed, not the child. He'd had her out on the sled, and he'd pulled her up the driveway. I can still hear him saying he'd only turned his back for a second. I looked at him and knew it was true. Having the kids here now, I understand even better. A second. A fraction of a second. They're so quick, those little ones." She shook her head. "It was a good thing it was so cold, they said. It slowed the bleeding."

He gave her shoulder a quick squeeze. "She came through, though. That's the important thing."

"She was so small, so still. They said I called 911. I don't remember that. Or covering her with my coat, I don't remember *that*, either. I remember how she looked and the way her father screamed, and how another man—a neighbor—kept him from moving her." She swallowed nothing. Her throat was dry. "She lost a leg. She was lucky, they said. She almost lost...a lot more. Her father had a hard time with it. Blamed himself."

"She's doing okay now?"

"She hates the prosthetic. She outgrows them so fast. But she's doing well in school. Plays the violin."

"So you keep in touch."

"It's a nice family. They've been through so much. I've almost been able to separate the child lying so still in the snow from the voice on the phone who tells me about her part in the school play."

"Almost?"

"It's the dreams."

He nodded. "Something bad happened. You can't change that. Sounds like that nice family has made their peace with it while you keep telling yourself you don't have the right. Why are you hangin' on to that child lying in the snow?"

"I'm not."

"That child lived and grew. She isn't the two-legged kid she might have been, true. She's the one who has a life and tells you about it."

"I know," she whispered, dry-eyed, her throat prickling. "I know. I'm glad she does. I don't want to think about that day. I try not to. There's a lot I don't even remember."

"I'm no psychiatrist, that's for sure. But I know something about self-inflicted wounds. They're twice as painful as any other kind."

She looked up at him. "Where's yours?"

"Same place as yours. In my head."

"And you don't like to talk about it either, do you?"

"I can't. I wish I could." He nodded toward the bunkhouse. "There's a bigger rock back there. Petrified wood, I think. Real pretty. I can't lift it, but I could drag it behind the pickup. It would look real nice out here in the yard somewhere."

"I know the one you mean." She patted his knee, an unconscious imitation of the woman who came immediately to mind. "Grandma used to call my grandfather the rock man. He brought them home from all over the place. That one is South Dakota petrified wood. There's more of it around. He was going to make something with his collection." She sighed. "I hardly remember him. We used to sit at the kitchen table and see who could eat the most ice cream. He scared me once when he caught me trying to open the chute on the grain bin. He told me never, never try to get into the grain bin. I was just trying to get some oats so I could get my pony to come to me."

"Yeah, I got in trouble for messing around in the shed where my dad stored oats. It looked like a mountain of stuff that was perfect for jumping into. There was a ladder—"

"Oh, God."

"He caught me in time." He smiled. "My father

did. My father who art in heaven with your grand-father. Right?"

"He died when I was five."

"What was his name?"

She raised an eyebrow. "Are you testing me?"

"Checking for Lakota blood." He smiled. "You think about where you want that rock, I'll move it for you."

They sat together without speaking as a long moment passed. "You offered to make repairs, but it sounds as though I'll be getting some real improvements," she said at last. "That storm must've been heaven-sent."

"Aren't they always?"

"I think I could sleep now. Will you come to bed with me?"

"No." He covered her hand with his. "I want you in *my* bed."

"It's a single bed. There's only room for one."

"Or two trying to be one." He kissed her fore-head, and then his lips feathered his promise against her skin. "I'll let you sleep. I'll just hold you."

He felt bone tired but muscle revived when he came out of the shower. He slipped into a pair of jeans, and she greeted him with a hand on his hip when he lay down beside her.

"Do you often sleep in your clothes?"

"No. But it'll be hard to just hold you if I'm not wearing anything."

"That was *your* plan." She snuggled against his chest. "I'm ready for that two-becoming-one trick."

"No tricks. I never want to trick you or deceive you about…" He drew a deep breath. "There's something you should know about me."

"I know all I need to." She knew all she *wanted* to. "You are—" she traced the shape of his flat areola with her finger "—a kind and gentle man. A cowboy. Granted, mothers always warn their daughters about cowboys, and I've always stayed away from them, but you…"

"I'm an ex-con." Her hand stilled. "Remember I told you I got arrested a couple of times?"

"You said the courts went easy on you."

"At first." He covered her hand with his as though he expected her to take it away. "I did time in the state pen for grand theft."

She swallowed hard. "How old were you?"

"Old enough. I wasn't a kid. I knew what I was doing. You wanna talk about guilt? That's what killed my father. Watching his son go to prison. I was gonna get everything back for him. That's what I told him anyway. I told him I was doing it for him. Worst lie I ever told in my life." His voice dropped to a low, secret register. Del had never spoken to anyone else about his crimes or the real reason he'd committed them.

He hated excuses. It was time for them to end. "I did it for myself. It made me feel like a big man. I was good at it, better than anybody I knew. That ain't sayin' much, of course, since they were all small-time thieves."

"Were you a big-time thief?" she asked quietly, and he stared at her. *Was she joking?* "Well, isn't that what grand theft is?"

"If it involves livestock, it's grand theft felony in this state." He paused. She was dead serious, and he had to give her all the truth he could. "I stole cattle."

"Oh." He could almost hear her processing the news. "How long ago?"

"I've been out for almost seven years."

"The ranchers you work for…don't know."

"When I was on probation, they knew. I had to report to a probation officer. Since then, well, nobody's asked."

"My father…"

He shook his head. "What do you think he'd say?"

"That you're a good hand."

"You think he'd trust me?"

She released a quick sigh. "He'd give you the benefit of the doubt."

"How about you? Do *you* trust me?" Her silence nearly killed him. "Lila?"

"As much as I did before. Maybe even more, since you get points for telling me. It's funny, isn't it? If I were going to hire you, I'd probably do a background check. But here I am, in bed with you. And I don't just do the two-trying-to-become-one thing with… I mean, I'm not easily impressed, and I don't let people… But you're very…"

"Kind and gentle?"

"Yes. Kind and gentle. And I feel like being kind and gentle back. Listening the way you do. Telling you secrets. Touching you. Being touched by you and no one else." She pressed her cheek against him. "Does that scare you?"

"No." He groaned. "Yeah, a little. I've never met anyone like you. I'm a big risk for you, and that scares me. I want to keep you safe." He pulled her into a twofer embrace. "I want to keep you, Lila. With me."

Chapter Eight

Del had a job to do. It was his real job, the one that really paid off, the one he enjoyed. He knew when he was closing in on something big. Brad had no idea what kind of deal they were mixed up in, but Del did. They were gofers at the bottom of a network of tunnels. Brad was anyway.

Del was a mole.

Brad was pumped when he pulled Del off the schoolhouse roof. It was twilight. Del had already decided to knock off at the end of the current row of shingles. He'd repaired the swings, fenced in the play yard, and he was bone tired. He didn't need a smashed thumb.

Brad's eyes glittered once he had Del riding shot-gun in his pickup. They were going to hit tribal cat-tle, he said. They had a man inside, and the pickings were fat. Adrenaline had turned Brad's mouth into a fountain of information.

"They won't *all* be tribal cattle," he said, as though he wanted to head off some imagined of-fense. "They've got a couple of places picked out. Indian ranchers running steers for big operations out of state. Gotta figure they won't miss a few head. Part of the cost of doing business. As for the tribe's cattle, hell, they get their stock on the government's dime anyway, right? Maybe some casino profits?"

"Yeah. Always have," Del said dismissively, but what he thought was, *Typical*. What Brad had both-ered to learn about the federal government's asso-ciation with tribal land—what was left of it—and how the Lakota Nation survived would fit on the head of a finish nail. "How long have you lived in Indian country, Brad?"

"Most of my life. But not on the reservation, of course. I mean, we butt right up to it, but they've got their land and we've got ours." Brad spared a glance toward the passenger seat. "You're from one of the reservations up north, right? Not that it mat-ters. This is a good deal, and you're smart enough to cut yourself in."

"Absolutely." Del stared at the road ahead. Not that *what* mattered? His willingness to steal from his cousins? His stomach churned, reminding him of the time when he had been.

"This outfit we're hooked up with, it's big. But they'll get in and get out. A couple more jobs and they'll disappear for a while. But they'll be back, and we'll be here."

"How did you get in with them?"

"Chet Klein hooked me up. You know Chet?"

"Heard the name," Del said, thinking back to his visit with Stan Chasing Elk. He had a mental file on Klein and he was ready to add to it.

"Yeah, you hear it a lot. If there's money to be had, Klein's got his hand out. Tribal college got a big grant for that agriculture program, and there was Chet, offering his services." Brad chuckled. "Made out like a bandit."

"Yeah? How'd he do that?" *Tell me more about this bandit than I already know.*

"You might say he's a facilitator. I took a couple of classes from him—my mother's idea, you know, impress Frank—and I got to know him pretty well. I'm not a tribal member, and neither is he, so when he'd 'borrow' stuff, I was the one he got to help run it out to his place. He told me right out to forget where we put it. Said nobody would ever ask me—tribal cops don't mess with white guys—but if anybody did, I should play dumb and then let him know." He shrugged. "Nobody ever asked me. No surprise, he got fired. I don't know what he did with all the stuff he took."

"How long have you been rustling? How many raids?"

"They just started working our area. I've set up a couple now, but there's a lot more to it. I know they find an isolated place where they can meet another truck, but I've never seen how they set up a rendez- vous, change the brands and all that."

"If they're good, they'll be in and out in the time it takes to pitch a round of horseshoes." Del smiled. They might come close, but no matter how good they were, he was better. "You pitch horseshoes?"

"No. Frank does, though. He's pretty good."

"You'll have to try it."

Close counted in horseshoes.

It was dark in the isolated draw several miles from the sign marking the reservation boundary. They were a little late to the party. If Brad was plan- ning on rising in the ranks, he was off to a bad start. Rustlers kept a schedule. Timing was everything, and everybody was expected to be on time. In and out, like clockwork. Del figured Brad was hearing about it from the hauler while he stood back wait- ing for his cue. The hauler was the driver, which put him in charge of the move. It was the hauler who signaled for Del to step up.

"Name's Chip," the hauler said as he handed Del a cattle prod.

Del nodded. "Fox."

"You know how to use this?"

"I do."

"You stand up there," Chip told Brad as he nodded toward a patch of prickly pear. "You let any get past you, you're done."

Del moved toward the trailer, where the cattle prod would come in most handy, but he watched the dog handler out of the corner of his eye. The same dogs were working this job as the last one. If the dogs were any indication, the outfit was making money somewhere. But if the man in charge could see the way the wrangler miscued his professionally trained herding dogs, it would be the man hitting the road. Not the dogs. The younger dog was barking his head off again because the stupid man didn't know how to use hand signals.

"Let me try." Del approached the handler when he could no longer stand to watch. He gestured for the bait.

"Don't I know you?" The man—yeah, he did seem familiar, Del thought—handed him a plastic sandwich bag containing dog treats.

Brad hung back the way he always did when there was work to be done, but he caught the man's question and edged closer. At this point it didn't matter. Let the word leak out. It proved Del's honor among thieves.

"Last name's Fox, right?" the guy said, his eyes lighting up. "I remember you now. We worked a few jobs together up in Missouri Breaks country, remember?" He patted his own chest. "Joe Clumer."

"Joe Clueless?" Del grinned. The nickname still fit. It wasn't often he ran into a guy who recognized him—the attrition rate was pretty high in the rustling business—but it happened.

"Damn. Heard you got sent up for, I don't know, was it rustling?" Clumer laughed. "What, you didn't get rehabbed?"

"Hard-core, I guess." Del whistled and gave a hand signal. The pair of blue heelers split up and double-teamed the recalcitrant steer threatening to cut loose. Between the snarling dogs and the trailer ramp, the choice for the steer was abundantly clear.

"You always was real good with the dogs. How long you been working for Pacer?"

"Just started." And just added a new mental file tabbed *Pacer*. Who was Pacer? Del knew he was being sized up. Brad had permission to bring him along. The rest was up to him, and he'd already made the right impression. He was the elusive Fox.

"We got a hell of an operation. You should see how fast we work the stock when we meet up."

Del stepped closer to his former compadre. "Can you get me in the truck?"

"Pacer likes to keep locals working the roundup side, but your friend's—"

As clueless as you are.

"I'm not local. Only been working at Benson's stepfather's place a couple weeks. I'm looking for something that pays better."

"I don't make any decisions around here. Word is Benson's got the same idea as you. Let me see what I can do. If I tell them I've seen you in action…"

"Whatever it takes to get me on."

Once the selected steers were loaded into the stock trailer, Clumer tried to get a cell phone signal. He finally had to take to higher ground, but he returned victorious.

"You're golden, Fox. Is there such thing? Red fox, gray fox. Is there such a thing as a golden fox?"

Del gave half a smile. "Like you said, you're lookin' at him."

"We're making one more haul this week. Pacer wants to fill the big trailer with Flynn's steers. Fifty head." Clumer clapped a beefy hand on Del's shoulder. It made him feel crawly. "You in?"

"What do I get out of it?"

"If you want in, that's what you get. *In.*"

Del nodded. "Why Double F steers?"

"Because they're ripe for picking. Benson's setting it up. It's gonna be fun. With a haul like that, we'll fix the brands right on-site." Clumer grinned. "These locals get us to the basket so we can score."

"When?"

"As soon as we take care of this load. Be ready."

Del motioned for Brad to vacate the driver's seat, and the hell with the fact that it was the little bastard's own pickup. He wanted to fill his hands with the steering wheel. Otherwise he'd be tempted to cold cock the kid before they got out on the highway. Brad complied without a word.

"What are you doing?" Del demanded. "The Double F has already been hit. Why risk a second raid? You're above suspicion."

He was also flying high on something. Del saw it in his eyes. He could only hope it was just adrenaline.

"You know that coulee in the corner of the north pasture?" Brad said. "About seven miles off the highway, so it's isolated, but there's easy access from the cut-across. They can set up right there on the cut-across. You move the steers into that coulee. It's perfect."

"You don't need to bring them into your backyard again. That's where you live, man. That's where you eat, where your family sleeps. What are you thinking?"

"Bigger haul and a bigger cut for us, man. You said it best. Thinking about getting something for myself. Nobody's gonna get hurt. They say the big man will probably be there, the one they call Pacer."

Brad shifted in his seat, angling toward Del. "You're thinking about getting a little something from pretty Miss Lila, aren't you, Fox? Hey, can't blame a guy for tryin'. I'd sure tap that." He chuckled. "If I had the time."

Time? Del set his jaw, put his tongue on lockdown and stared at the road ahead. *A hundred years wouldn't even get you close.* That thought and a long, deep breath kept him steady.

"All right, Brad. We'll play in your backyard."

Though *playing* wasn't exactly what he had in mind.

Del was already working the hay field at sunrise. He would have the storm-soaked windrows turned by dinnertime. An afternoon of hot Dakota sun would go a long way toward preparing the field for the baler. Frank showed up a little while later with the same idea, but Del had beaten the old man to the punch, which Frank acknowledged with a wave of approval before heading out to finish mowing. Del wished he could be around to help bale up the hay. For the moment he was exactly the man he'd claimed to be—a good hand—and he liked it. For the moment.

He worked all morning, then skipped dinner at the Flynn house. He didn't feel like talking. The rocks he'd carted up to Lila's flower bed beckoned. The sun was merciless, which was fine. He wasn't looking for mercy. He wanted cleansing heat. Fire power. He could hear children's voices, and he knew there was shade in the play yard he'd repaired for them. He smiled when Lila's voice mixed with theirs in song as they played an age-old game. He had a circle forming around the flower bed, and he imagined the little circle she was making with the kids. He glanced over at the patch of shade behind the corner of the house where Asap lay watching his human bake himself in the summer sun. Was that pity in those puppy eyes? Or prudence?

More likely common canine sense.

It made little human sense for Del to imagine what his bookcases would look like finished and filled with books, or how the old schoolhouse windows would hardly look any different once he'd weatherized them. He could bring that sweet old building up to anybody's code, even his father's. The old man would be pleased to know how much his son had learned from him, how eager he was to put that handed-down know-how to use. *You might not care, Delano, but someday your wife will.* Del had turned his teenage nose up at the idea of a someday wife or a future home. But it turned out that some part of him had tuned in.

And for today that meant something. He was building a rock garden for the first woman he'd ever imagined as his wife. For today he was simply her father's hired hand—a good man aspiring to become a better one, dreaming of building a life with the boss's daughter. Unlikely as it sounded, it was a possibility today. Tomorrow—or maybe the next day—it would not be. How could it? He would be facilitating a theft at the Double F. A net would be cast, and people were going to get caught. As always, the net would yield some surprises.

The pup stirred from his spot in the lengthening shade.

"What are you two up to, Ace?"

"Stay there," Del called out at the sound of Lila's voice. She stood at the far corner of the house, where she could still keep an eye on the kids, fists resting on her sweet hips.

"Me or the dog?"

"Both. *Stay.*" He laughed as he mopped his face with the bandanna he'd tucked in his back pocket and started toward her. "I'll come to you. This isn't ready for your inspection."

"Inspection? Oh, how exciting" She glanced over her shoulder, checking the play yard. "You have a surprise for me, don't you? The kids and I are going in pretty soon for cookies and lemonade. Would you care to join us?" She started baby talking Asap. "You, too, Ace. You want some water?" She reached down to pet him, and the dog's tail started spinning like a pinwheel. "You want a cookie? I have a cookie for you. Oh, yes, I do."

"We're good. We both have water."

"But you don't have cookies," she chirped as she turned toward the play yard again. She'd left the gate open, and her tone shifted from birdsong to drill sergeant. "Rocky, put your tennis shoes back on."

"I have to warn you, I took out the plants that looked dead," Del said as he strode from sun to shade at the back of the house. "Which was most of them."

"I know. Between Brad's pickup and the storm…"

"The good news is you can put new stuff in. It's shaped a little different. You'll probably want different stuff." God, he wanted to greet her properly. Even a quick kiss would go a long way toward twilight, when he planned to walk with her. Simply stroll hand in hand the way lovers were supposed to. "I don't know much about flowers. I know my rocks, but flowers are a woman's special…thing."

"Will you have supper with me tonight?" She smiled, her eyes twinkling. "I think you'll like my special recipe for 'Trail Rider's Hot Dish.'"

"I can't wait."

"I can't, either. But I guess we'll—"

"Lila, Rocky won't…"

They turned quickly like two guilty kids. And there stood the third kid.

Little Denise. "Is this your boyfriend, Lila?"

"How did you guess?"

"By the way you're looking at each other." Denise gave Del an imperial once-over. "Are you supposed to be here? Because my sister has a boyfriend, and he isn't supposed to come around my sister when she's working."

"Question is, where are *you* supposed to be?" Del softened the challenge with a wink and a smile. "Cut us a little slack, huh? We work, too."

"Del built the new fence and fixed the swings after the storm knocked them down."

"And now I'm fixing up the flower bed on the side of the house." Del flashed Lila a smile. "And my boss just told me it's almost time for cookies and lemonade."

"You're her boyfriend and she's your boss?"

"I'm nobody's boss but mine." Lila folded her arms. "And that's the way I like it."

"But Rocky won't stop—ouch!" A small green tomato bounced off the back of Denise's head. She whirled, stomped her foot and shook her finger. "Rocky Rhoades, you stop throwing stuff."

"Rocky Rhoades?" Del slid Lila a *seriously?* look, and she confirmed with a smile.

"You're not the boss of me!" Denise told Rocky vehemently.

"Whoa, Rocky," Del said, grinning.

"I'm nobody's boss but mine, and you are not my boyfriend!" Denise shouted.

"Hey," Del said. "I've got the perfect job for you, my man. You wanna help me? No girls, no bosses." He glanced up at Lila. "Call us when you've got the cookies ready." He took the little boy's hand and headed toward the corner of the house. "Is Taylor Rhoades your dad?"

"Yeah. You know my dad?

"I do. Quite a sense of humor he's got."

"What do you mean, sense of humor?"

"He tells great stories. My dad was like that, too. Told some whoppers, my dad did."

"Is he still, like…"

"Still with me? He sure is. I don't say his name, but I tell his stories." He tapped his hand against his thigh. "Come with the boys, Ace."

"Why don't you say his name?"

"Because…"

When Paula Rhoades arrived, Rocky grabbed her hand, made a beeline toward the driveway, took a sudden right-angle turn and skidded to a halt beside the garden he'd helped build. He was pointing out the rocks he liked best, reporting how he'd helped Del switch this one with that one because they were too heavy for one person, and where Lila was going to put the special flowers for the butterflies. Del enjoyed the whole spiel, partly for the kid's enthusiasm and partly for the smile on Lila's face as they caught up to mother and child.

"And nobody better try to run over these rocks. Anybody who does has got rocks in their head, 'cuz Del and me worked really hard." Rocky pointed to a pinkish boulder. "That's granite. When we washed everything, some of them sparkled. I get to help water the plants, and Denise doesn't."

"You get to show the others how to water," Lila reminded him.

"Yeah, and Denise doesn't get to boss me."

"Sounds like you had a good day." Paula nodded at Del. "I didn't get a chance to meet you at the dance. I'm Taylor's wife. He's talked you up, too. Wanted me to meet you, but seems like you left early."

Del nodded toward Rocky. "You've got the makings of a good landscaper here."

"He's just like his father—all boy. He sure likes Lila." She smiled at her son. For Del she had a more purposeful look. "We all do."

"She got hit hard by the storm," Del said. "Tore up the kids' play yard pretty bad, but we fixed it up."

"Well, good," Paula said. "You sure made a nice flower bed here."

"*We* did it, Mom. It's called Rocky's Rockery."

"Thanks. I just…wanted to say how nice it was to see—" she grabbed Rocky's hand "—Lila get to go to the dance."

"It was nice to see *you* there, too, Paula. It's been a while for me," Lila said. "I'm such a homebody."

"That's me, too. Once you get to a party like that, you never know what'll happen."

"Mom," Rocky piped up. "Lila has a boyfriend, and you know who it is? It's Del."

"Rocky! That's none of your... Who said that? Your dad?"

"Denise guessed, and Lila said how did she guess."

Paula looked surprised when Lila laughed. "I'd better get him home," she said.

Lila turned to Del as the last car of the day sped toward the highway, dust trail fluttering from the bumper like rust-colored sheets flapping on the line.

"I'll bet you think that was weird."

"No, I don't. I know her husband."

"You think I'm a little weird, too, huh?"

Del smiled. "No, I don't. I know your boyfriend." She laughed, and he added, "And I know small towns. People see things, they think they know things and they talk. I didn't mean to embarrass you."

"I don't get embarrassed."

"I didn't mean to hurt you. I don't ever want to cause you trouble, Lila. That's the last thing I want. The last..."

He took her shoulders in his hands and pulled her closer for a kiss thorough enough to erase the word *last* from his mind, at least for a while. He came away smiling.

That night he stuck with his plan. After a delicious supper—damn, that woman could cook—

they watched the sun set and walked through tall buffalo grass along the pasture fence line during the magic hour, the time when daylight was softened by coming nightfall, meadowlarks tweedled in the grass and crickets let it be known that they would be taking over now. Del surprised Lila with a pallet of blankets and South Dakota sage, fresh cut and pungent, which made for especially sweet lovemaking. They were surrounded by a black velvet sky overrun with stars that brightened when they touched each other and danced with them when they soared together.

Spent and content, they held each other and marveled at the way they had shifted the heavens and moved the stars. They whispered back and forth, back and forth, like water softly lapping earth's still body, while the smell of sage helped the night breeze chase mosquitoes away.

"Have you ever been in love before?" she asked because she dared, because she must have known his answer would not, *could* not, detract from what they were feeling.

"Not like this."

"Not like what?"

"Not like I am now. With you." He nuzzled her hair. He hated lying, and this was one thing he wouldn't lie about. When she found out what he was up to, she would never believe him again, but right now, in this moment, he wanted her to know the deepest, brightest, most important truth he had in him. "I'm not a boy who's crazy over a girl or a piece of a man looking for a way to get through the night. I'm a whole man in love with a whole woman."

"Wow." Her face, washed in starlight, was open and innocent of color. "You take me by surprise at every turn." She smiled. "In a good way."

"Not always."

It wouldn't feel like a good way, not for long. If she loved him back, she wasn't going to enjoy the surprise he had waiting for her. It was already in place, right around the next turn. If she loved him, it was going to hit her hard.

She gave him an odd glance, then went on. "But you know what really surprises me? I can handle that. You know? Take a chance, Lila," she instructed herself. "Life isn't always any particular thing. It comes with surprises." She touched the tip of her nose to his cheek and whispered, "I've never been in love before, and I never expected to be."

"You didn't expect me. And I sure as hell didn't expect you." He pressed his lips against the top of her ear and ran the tip of his tongue inside the delicate curve. She giggled, and he felt her joy deep in his gut. It hurt. He closed his eyes, rested his forehead on her crown and whispered, "You're the right woman at the wrong time."

"How can there be a wrong time to love the right woman?"

He groaned. "It's complicated."

"Of course it is. You're complicated. Fortunately, I'm not. So lay it on me." She popped up suddenly, propping herself on her elbow. "Wait. Are you married? Because if that's your next surprise, you won't like the way I handle it."

He laughed. "You're a pistol, you know that?"

"I'm not, and I don't have one. But I can get one in a hurry."

"I'm not married, and I never have been." He rubbed her bottom lip with the pad of his finger. "Everything I've told you about myself is true. But there's one more thing. And I can't get into that with you. I just...can't."

She lay down again—flopped back a little too hard, sounded like—folded her arms and stared at the sky for a moment.

"Now what do we do?" She wasn't whispering anymore. "Play Twenty Questions?"

"Now you trust me. Or you don't." He had to take back something he'd once said to her. A long time ago, seemed like. A different life. "Actions can be deceiving. Sometimes explanations *do* matter, but I can't give you one yet."

"You haven't gone back to your former profession, have you?"

"I'm not a thief." He took her chin in his hand

and turned her to face him. "Believe that, okay? No matter what."

"Do *you* have a pistol? Because if you were convicted and went to prison…"

One corner of his mouth rose. "The only thing that stops a bad man with a gun is a good man with—"

"Which one *are* you, Del?"

"Some of each, I guess. But without a gun. I never pack a gun."

"Because…"

"Because I don't wanna get killed." He sealed that big truth with a kiss and then added another equally big truth. "Even more important, I don't want you to get hurt."

"This is—"

"No more questions. Trust me." He touched her bottom lip again, this time with his thumb. "You're not sleeping with the enemy, Lila. I promise."

He took her in his arms and blessed her moment of silence.

Short-lived though it was.

"I can't sleep. Will you answer just one question?"

"If I can."

"What's your name?"

"Delano Fox. I guess it was Takes The Fox, but they changed it somewhere along the line." He chuckled. "Maybe it was Steals The Fox. Maybe I come from a long line of thieves."

"You were a thief, but you aren't anymore, and your name really is Del."

He kissed her eyes closed, one at a time. "When we make love, do you think I want you callin' out a name that ain't mine?"

Chapter Nine

Del wondered if Asap thought he'd treed some kind of prey. If sawdust could be called a tree and a chirping cricket qualified as prey, then the pup was a true hunter. He turned off the table saw, brushed tree shavings from the smooth plank and examined his cut.

"These are gonna be real nice, Del." Frank had come out to see if he wanted supper and stayed to check out the first bookcase as though he was thinking about buying it. "You've got a knack for woodwork. I can handle the basics, but when you want a nice finish 'cuz you want to be able to put something inside the house, I'm not your man. I bought all those tools. Whenever I come across a deal on a tool I don't have, I put it in the cart."

"But some of them you've never used."

"I was always gonna get around to it when I got caught up. But you never get caught up in this business. Maybe not in this life. When you're young, there's always something else you want. You get old, there's a lot more you want to do." Frank leaned his butt against the workbench, adjusted his Short Straw Co-Op cap by the bill and folded his arms over his barrel chest. "What do *you* want, Del?"

"I'm gettin' along pretty good with what I've got. All I was missing were woodworking tools, and now…" His sweeping gesture took in Frank's table saw, jigsaw, sanders and more.

"You seem to be getting along pretty good with my daughter."

Del wasn't about to touch that one.

"I'm glad." Frank drew a deep breath. "Not that it's any of my business. I mean, I don't meddle. Lila keeps to herself. I think I told you, she owns half the ranch. The land anyway."

He wasn't going to touch that one, either.

"It's hard work, and it's a roller-coaster business. But you know that."

"I know the work. The business side is the boss's worry."

"Brad for sure ain't cut out for it."

Del stacked the plank with three others just like it. He hoped he would have time to sand that last edge.

"I know you haven't been around this family too long, but long enough. A man like you, you figured us out pretty quick."

Us? He had Benson figured out pretty quick, but *us?*

No. Not possible. He *had* been around this family long enough, and it was Benson. Just Benson.

But Frank was standing there with a look in his eyes that said he had something on his mind and he was trying to decide whether it was time to let Del in on it.

Ordinarily he would be all ears. He wouldn't look the man in the eye, but he would nod at the right time, maybe offer a word or two of encouragement, get him to keep it coming. Times had been tough, money was tight, all he had to do was look the other way while the boy, the mother, the wife…

But this wasn't his usual assignment. When had he ruled Frank out? Right about now Del wished he wore a hearing aid with a mute button. He eyed the power saw longingly, but it would be rude to turn it on now, and there was nothing to cut anyway.

"I ain't ready to quit," Frank was saying. "Sure, I've had a few medical problems, but I'm not that damn feeble. All I need is a good hand to help out. Guys like you are hard to find. Hell, that last bum Brad hired was useless. You could just tell he wasn't gonna be around long." Frank shifted his weight, switched the way he'd had his ankles crossed. "Are you?"

"Am I what?"

Frank cleared his throat and then allowed a precious moment of silence to pass. "My wife wants me to turn the place over to Brad."

"And you're not ready."

"I'll never be ready. He'd run it into the ground so fast…" He shook his head and blew a deep sigh. "I don't want to go live in Florida, but I could take her on that boat ride or whatever kind of trip she's so anxious to take if I had somebody here I knew I could depend on." Another firm adjustment of the cap. "No, sir, Brad's not gettin' this place."

Was it time to breathe a sigh of relief?

"If you're asking me what his plans might be, I can't—"

"I don't care what his plans are. I don't think he has any. I guess I'm asking you what *your* plans are."

Oh, jeez. Frank would know soon enough. Ordinarily Del would slip out the door, content with the knowledge that the bad people would get their day in court and their years behind bars, while the good people would… Okay, sure, they might be in for some rough days, depending on the circumstances, but they were good people, sturdy stock. They would put their lives back together and move on.

And so would he.

"I like my job here."

"And my daughter? You like *her*, too, don't you?"

He swallowed hard, nodded once. "I do."

"See, that's what I like about you, Del. There's no beating around the bush with you." This time the precious pause was pregnant. "So are you two, uh…?"

Speaking of boat trips, Del's hard glance was a shot across the bow. *Now's the time to chug off, Frank.*

"I just mean, with all the work you've been doing for her—and I appreciate it, because I offer, and she says she can handle it herself, but you're putting in extra time—hell, all that extra work, you must be—"

"I don't mind."

"So you're doing it for Lila."

"I went out and checked the alfalfa." It was the answer to the kind of question the boss actually had a right to ask. "The field's dried out pretty good."

"Like I said, you're a good hand. I'd like to keep you around. I think Lila would like that, too."

Del chuckled. "And you'd also like to keep *her* around."

"If it's what she wants, I'd like it very much if she stayed." Frank slowly shook his head. "I don't know what she wants. She keeps to herself. She had that accident— I mean, I know it was bad, but she never talks to us about it. Scared her so bad she stopped driving. I know that. I know it wasn't her fault. No charges or anything. But I *don't* know…" He looked at Del. It was the look of a man who cared enough to swallow his pride. "She tell *you* about it?"

"Some."

"She stayed up there in Minnesota for months after it happened. We thought she'd finished college. Found out later she didn't. I was pretty damn pissed about that, but she never explained herself. Not to me anyway. Maybe to the Chasing Elks." He lifted one shoulder. "Yeah, probably."

"She didn't have to explain herself to them. Or to me."

"Tell you what, when I was growing up, I sure as hell had to explain *my*self. If I'da had the chance to go to college, and if I'da got so far and then walked away…"

Frank slapped his palm on the workbench. Del wasn't sure what that meant, but he *was* sure he wasn't going to ask.

"Did you go to college?" Frank asked finally.

"Hard Knocks U," Del said.

"Now, there's a degree that can open doors or close 'em."

"It does both. Gives you some options."

"That's why Lila went away, I guess. Looking for options. This place is all I have, and she owns half of it. It's not a bad option."

Del nodded, but he had nothing of his own to add to the conversation, and he wasn't about to contribute anything that belonged to Lila.

"I shouldn't be butting into her business," Frank said.

Del raised his brow and agreed with a nod.

Frank chuckled. "When I was younger I had all kinds of plans for this place, for Lila, maybe even for Brad, if he'd been interested in learning something. I'm running the School of Hard Work here."

Del smiled. "You've got a fine campus."

"Yeah." Frank beamed. "Yeah, I do. What is it they say about life happening while you're making other plans? It's true." He pushed away from the workbench. "I want my daughter to be happy. Whatever it takes, I'm all for it."

"Have you told her that?"

"She knows."

"I bet she'd like to hear you say it." Del shook his head and chuckled. "Now we're both acting like we know what Lila wants."

"Even when a woman tells you she wants something, she's only giving you one little corner of the picture. There's always more to it, but she expects you to get the big picture off that one corner."

"A cruise ship is big, Frank." Del grinned. Frank scowled. "Complete package," Del explained. "Total picture, nothing left out. And come on. June hasn't been too subtle about drawing it up for you."

"You been on a cruise?"

"Nope."

"Well, I want June to be happy, too, but I can't leave this place in Brad's hands, not even for a week. And that's what she wants. She thinks Brad could take over the Double F." Frank folded his arms again. "What do you think?"

"That kind of thinking is above my pay grade, Frank."

"You've been to Bucky's with him a few times, haven't you? Hanging out with the local boys?" Frank cocked his head, trying to look into Del's eyes and draw a bead on the truth. "Anybody else ever come around? Anybody who's not from around here?"

"Besides me?"

"Yeah, besides you. Somebody who smells like stolen cattle."

"Sure seems like this area's been mapped out by prairie pirates." Del started hanging tools up on wall pegs. "Rustling's become a big problem everywhere. Nobody's safe."

"You talking about places you've worked?"

"Everywhere. But yeah, they caught some rustlers where I was working out in Colorado not long ago. They'd come up from Texas, but they had a young guy working with them who was local. Stealing from his neighbors."

"You make an insurance claim, they pay up eventually, but then they drop you. I hate dealing with insurance companies. It's a racket. But then, so's rustling." Frank cleared his throat. Seemed as if he had to be making some kind of noise when he was taking aim. "You never answered my question, Del. You don't seem like the kind of a man who'd cover for somebody."

"Cover for somebody?" Del flashed Frank an incredulous look. "That's not where I thought your questions were leading."

"Brad's always been one to test the limits, you know? He's gotten himself into a few tight spots. Took a car and drove it into a river when he was in high school."

"*Your* car?"

"Would've been a hell of a lot easier if it was. I had to pay for the car and call in some favors to keep him out of court. That wasn't the only time. He's the kind of kid who really needs to pay the price for a lesson, and I—" he rolled his eyes "—can't say no to his mother."

"You think Brad's rustling cattle?"

"I don't know. I hope not. Like I said, he doesn't have the makings of a rancher. He's all hat and no horse. He did a little baling this afternoon, spent most of his time and mine pulling out twine he'd screwed up when he tried to splice it. Can't even make a square knot, that kid. He's a jack of *no* trades, as far as I can tell. He'd no more build some-

thing like this in his spare time than peel a grape."
Frank laid a beefy hand on one of the bookcases.
"Has Lila seen this?"

"I wanted to have one finished before I showed
her. This one's ready to be painted. Shelves are ad-
justable, see?" He lifted the top shelf to show off
the support pegs. He'd become a pretty good carpenter at Hard Knocks U. "The other two are ready
to be put together. Just look at this one to see how
the pieces all fit."

A long moment passed.

"Are you leaving?"

"That wouldn't be my choice, Frank, but in my
line of work, you never know."

"What *is* your line of work, Del?" Frank asked
quietly.

"Jack of many trades, like most cowboys." Del
ran his hand over the smooth shelf. "Brad hired
me. I appreciate that." He looked Frank in the eye.
"What's between Lila and me is personal, but right
here you can see…" He stepped back and gave an
openhanded gesture. "I'm all for books and librar-
ies, but this isn't my contribution to any cause. I care
for Lila. Whatever happens, I want you to know that.
I want *her* to know that."

Whatever was about to happen. Wheels were
turning, trucks were rolling and people were on
their way. The Double F was about to be hit, and

with any luck Del would meet the man behind the plan. He'd driven up on the hill he was beginning to think of as his personal phone booth, conferred and confirmed. Now he would wait for Brad to pick him up.

As he approached the bunkhouse, he stiffened. He couldn't have left the light on in his room. It had been midafternoon when he'd stopped in for his phone and his ID, both hidden in the old dresser with the swollen drawers, one of which he'd made impossible for anybody but him to open, and he hadn't been back since. There were times when he regretted not having a gun. A nice little .22 pistol would come in handy right about now.

Or not. The conceal part of conceal and carry could be damn tricky for a cowboy. A .22 was made for strapping into a holster.

So he took a peek in the window and scoffed at himself when his heartbeat tripped into overdrive. Oh, he had it bad for the woman sitting on the floor beside his bed. He could only see part of her face, but he would know those pretty feet and that sassy rooster-tail hairdo anywhere. He signaled Asap to stay back while he snuck around the corner and barged through the door. He barely got a squeak out of her, but Asap started yapping his head off and rushed to somebody's defense. Probably hadn't decided whose.

Lila shook her head and gave him that sweet look

that made a man feel like a kid again—the look that had once made him try whatever trick he had in his repertoire just so he could coax it from a pretty girl. The look that said, *You're the one.*

She was sitting in the middle of the makings of her own major project.

"What's all this?"

"I ordered it from that Swedish furniture company. It's supposed to be good quality, and you put it together yourself, so you save money." She waved a piece of paper at him. Instructions, unless he missed his guess. He would have left those in the box. "It's a new dresser. I know the drawers on the old one are a real pain. The top one, especially."

"Did you get it open?" He was taking a mental inventory. The case file, photos. She couldn't have opened it, but she might have noticed that it wasn't just hard to open, it was impossible—impossible unless you knew where the shim was anyway.

"Why would I want to open your drawers?"

He smiled.

"The directions are just pictures. The first part went together pretty easily, but these drawers…"

He watched her take two pieces of blond wood in hand and put tongue to groove. It was going to be a tight fit. She held her breath and pressed, let go with a sigh and groaned, leaned back against the side of the bed and scowled at the resisting parts. Then she took them in hand again, clearly determined to make them fit together. She took a firm grip and growled at the stubborn joint while she pushed until her hands shook. On the next attempt she tried a high-pitched squeal.

"Does it help?"

She looked up from her struggle. "What?"

He was pretty sure his imitation of her growls and squeals was spot on, but she wasn't laughing. He found an empty patch of floor and squatted on his heels amid parts piled together by shape and size. She'd sorted bolts and screws by size and type in a muffin tin. As he scanned the inventory, he heard the two pieces snap together. He looked up and enjoyed her self-satisfied smile.

"The squeaky wheel gets the job done," she said.

He smiled back. "The squeaky wheel gets the grease is the way I heard it."

"And then gets the job done. It takes elbow grease. The grease primes the elbows, and then you…" She stuck her elbows out, butted her fists together and pushed, reprising her grunts and groans. At the edge of the sprawl sat Asap, whining as he cocked his head side to side. "Yes, boys, every woman is born with the knowledge that a little noise helps move things along."

"Don't be giving away too many female secrets so early in the game," Del warned as he seated himself on the floor and picked up the directions. Asap flopped in place.

"The proof is in the pudding."

"We don't have any pudding yet." He perused the drawing on the paper and glanced at the frame. "Looks to me like we've got upside-down cake. One side's upside down."

"No, the directions show…" She scooted up behind him, rested her chin on his shoulder and reached around him to point to the paper. "See, this little guy is holding side A? And his wife is facing him with side B, so if you imagine them side by side—"

"How do you know that's his wife?"

"The wife gets the wavy hair. The dresser is for their kid's bedroom, obviously, because it's not big enough for the parents, even though they wear the same clothes, same size and everything." She patted his denim-clad thigh. "Just like us. Anyway, I pretended I was her, and then I pretended I was him, and I figured out the way they're holding the boards, so you have to turn—"

"Honey, we're looking at it head-on." He held the paper up for comparison. She moved her hand to his belly. He smiled to himself. "Does that look like it's sitting level to you? Did you have to force it?"

"A little. I've never made anything from a kit before."

"I'm bettin' it's the left side that's upside down." He turned his head toward her and smiled. "If it doesn't fit, it ain't time to quit."

She slid her hand over his belt buckle and rested it on his fly. "Would you help me make it fit?"

He reached around back of her head, released the big clip, freed her hair and plunged his fingers into it as he drew her mouth to his. She rubbed him, squeezed him gently, made his jeans feel tight and his head feel light. He canted his head for a second approach, a slip of the tongue, and she took the opportunity to slide into his lap, barely disturbing their kiss as she straddled him.

"I'll help you," he whispered. "I'll take you and make you over. Hold you upside down, turn you inside out." He kissed her neck, took her bottom in his hands and pulled her in, dragging her along the aching ridge in his lap. "Make me fit. I want to live inside you, Lila. I want to build my home in you." She answered with tremulous breaths and undulating hips. "I'm in love with you," he said, desperate to be loved back.

"Oh, my God, Del. I don't dare."

"Dare. You're a brave woman. You said it once." He leaned back far enough to read her eyes, to show her the depth of his need. "Tell me again. Now. Tonight."

"I've loved you since…" She glanced at the ceiling and back again. "Since you brought Asap."

"But you didn't know it then."

"I felt it. Something I've never felt before, and it

just keeps—" she rocked her hips, kissed him hard, rested her forehead against his "—growing."

He gripped her hips and rose to meet her, to kiss her and hold her against him and make her feel more.

And then came the unwelcome knock on the door.

"Hey in there, you decent?"

"Damn." He kissed her again, quickly, just one more kiss.

"Hey, Fox, it's time."

"I'll be out in a minute."

She'd slipped off his lap, and now she slid her hand down his arm and grabbed his hand. "Stay," she whispered.

"I can't."

"Why not? What's Brad talking about? Time for what?"

"Just…I said I'd go along."

"Along with what?" Suddenly wide-eyed with alarm she should have no reason to feel, she shook her head. "Don't go, Del. Stay with me."

"I can't. He hired me, Lila. If I'm gonna come back to you, I have to go now."

"You *don't* have to go with him. You've put in your day's work. This is our time, yours and mine." When he failed to speak, the look in her eyes cooled. "Choose."

"Take care of Asap, okay?" He touched his lips to

her forehead and said softly, "I choose you, I swear. But I have to go."

"Hey, what's…?" The door opened, and there stood Brad, grinning as though he'd found his sister's diary. "Well, hey, Lila."

Del got to his feet and offered her a hand, which she ignored.

"You guys can finish your project later, huh?" Brad cocked a forefinger at Del. "We've got a party to go to."

"Do you have room for one more?"

Lila drew surprised looks from both men.

"Not this time," Brad said. "It's kind of a bachelor party, and we don't want to be late."

"Are you going to Bucky's?" she asked.

Del put his arm around her shoulders and drew her to him. She neither obliged nor resisted. "I want to take you somewhere nice, just the two of us," he whispered. She looked up at him as though she'd given up on making sense of him. "You make a plan, okay?" He leaned close to her ear. "Remember what I said."

Chapter Ten

"She was dyin' to come with us, you could just tell," Brad said as they sped down the highway.

What was the guy's problem? Del wondered. Didn't he know silence was golden leading up to go time? If he had to be all hyped and chatty, he should have been talking about the job. But he was as dense as granite.

"She's like the icicle hanging on to the house. Look but don't touch. What'd you do to warm her up, man?"

None of your damn business.

"You got a call about tonight?"

"A text," Brad said. "Two, in fact. They're on their way, and they want us out there."

Now you're on the right track, kid.

"I took a run out there after I got the first text saying we should be ready," Brad said. "The steers you moved the other day are still in the coulee, right where we want them. Haven't budged, like they're waiting for their ride to show up. So I texted back." He chuckled. "Then I made a mess of the baler. Kept Frank busy all afternoon. You cut the fence on the west side?"

"Hell no. Turn to page one, Brad. You're making it too complicated. This is gonna be the biggest job you've seen yet, and it has to move fast."

"Yeah, but when it's all over, we'll still be here. It looks better if there's a fence down, doesn't it?"

"Just use the gate. It's down. We just fixed it but now it's down again. Damn beeves must've busted through again. Then the cops want to know, how long has it been like that? When was the last time you checked that pasture, Mr. Benson?"

Brad finally got the message. "We don't know when it happened. My hired hand regularly takes care of that, and I thought he was still on top of it, but I guess we got our signals crossed. Dad's had him putting up hay the last week or so, so it could've happened any time during the last week."

"Leave Frank out of it," Del said. "He's got nothing to do with it."

"He's about to lose fifty head. He'll have plenty to say about it. So will Lila. That's her land."

"I'll fix what's broken if you don't fire me for not doing my job."

"Fire you? Why would I do that? You're a valuable man, Mr. Fox. Living up to your name. I'm keeping you around." Brad laughed. "When this is over you can go steppin' out someplace nice with my stepsister. Just the two of you." He was so pleased with himself, he couldn't quit. "Doing your own little two-step."

Lila sat on the side of Del's bed, her heart pounding. The night was hot, and the air was heavy with bad energy. There was no point in cleaning up the mess she'd made in the bunkhouse. He wasn't coming back tonight. Maybe ever. Brad was up to something, which was nothing new. Either Del was in on it, or he was about to find himself neck deep in trouble. He'd wanted to hear her say the words, say them now, *tonight*, but he couldn't stay with her, had to go with Brad, had to go now, *tonight*. Stolen cattle, ex-con, former cattle rustler. *Ex. Former.* The pieces fit together too easily in her mind, but her heart kept pulling them apart.

He was walking into something, or he was already in on it. She had to know which it was.

The keys were in his pickup. She *had* to know, and this was the only way to find out. She opened the door with a trembling hand, and the dog jumped in ahead of her.

"Oh, no, Ace, you can't go. I'll probably start at the bar. You don't want to go there. Come on." She gave a noisy air kiss. She wasn't sure she what was going to happen after she turned the key, and she couldn't risk anybody's neck but her own. "Come. I'll put you…" The yard light put a gleam in the dog's black eyes as he cocked his head as if to say, *What are you waiting for, woman?*

"You should be buckled in," she muttered as she climbed behind the wheel. "I don't know what I'm doing. I don't drive anymore. I don't even remember how to…

"Of *course* I do. Stop being a ninny, woman. Just—" All it took was a turn of the key and a shift of the gears. Just like riding a bike. "Do it."

No traffic, no headlights except for hers. Del's. His pickup, his dog, his trouble. She was crazy for trying to follow. She wasn't sure where they were going, but she had a feeling it wasn't Bucky's Place. The population might be sparse, but the miles were many, the prairie nearly endless. Still, there was only one road to Short Straw. She might be on a fool's errand, but at least she wasn't sitting at home. There was a chance she would catch up, she told herself.

Keep your eyes open.

And suddenly, there it was—a state patrol car

parked at the turn to the cut-across. It was as good a sign as any. She couldn't imagine who'd called or how they'd gotten there so fast, but this was the scene of the earlier crime. Did that make it ripe for another picking? Lila calculated nothing but the amount of room she would need to make her turn. "Hang on, Ace. We're going in."

She blew past the Statie and hit the dirt road with a furor. The siren she expected didn't materialize. Maybe they realized she was on her own land. She'd spent half her youth driving these rutted back roads and the other half bouncing along in the passenger seat.

"You might want to get down on the floor, Ace." She glanced in the side mirror. She was okay so far, as long as she didn't fishtail. She'd grown up driving these roads. She could do this.

Paws on the dash, nose to the windshield, Asap whined.

"Down!" The dog flopped flat on the seat. "Amazing. In no time at all he has a stray dog and a crazy woman eating out of his hand, doing tricks, chasing after him like two…"

She could see lights several miles down the road, especially bright since she'd turned hers off. Especially crazy since she was barreling through the dark. The sight was like a September scene, when big trucks and tractors might run all night to bring in the fall crop or ship cows, or haul hay.

Wrong season, though, she thought. Wrong rigs. Loose cattle, men darting around, pushing, shouting. The gate was down, so she plowed through, then slowed down so no one would hear her coming. She parked safely outside the ring of light but close enough to see what was going on. There was a big one-ton pickup parked beside a huge stock trailer. She could hear cattle bawling, the sound echoing within the metal confines, smell the familiar acrid odor of burning hide and hair.

Branding? In all this mess, had somebody been branding cattle?

She counted at least five cars, with another one closing in behind her. It was a crazy scene. Only a lunatic would get out of the pickup and become part of it. But she rolled down the driver's window partway, told Asap to stay put and marched into the thick of it, heading straight for a man getting himself handcuffed. She would know that silhouette anywhere.

"Jesus, Lila, what are you doing here?"

"That's a good question," said the cop with the cuffs.

"I had to see for myself."

"Who are you?" the cop demanded.

"She's the land owner," Del said without looking away from her. With his arms behind his back, his hat gone, his hair hanging practically to his eyes, he looked almost boyish. "Her father owns the steers. They have nothing to with this."

"The owners have everything to do with it, especially when they know when and where it's going down."

"She didn't." He tried to step closer to her, but the cop jerked him back. "What are you doing here, Lila?"

"What are *you* doing here? *Why*, Del? I thought this was all behind you."

"Remember what I said."

"What you *said*? What I *see* is my father's cattle, somebody else's trailer, a bunch of police cars on *my* land and you wearing handcuffs. That sort of negates everything you've *said*."

He glanced past her. "You drove my pickup." He allowed her a half smile. "Lila, you drove. Good for you."

"Good for… Are you serious?"

One of the stock dogs started snarling at one of the men—good man or bad, Lila couldn't tell at this point. Asap poked his head and paws through pickup window and launched a blistering protest.

"You brought Asap?"

"He insisted."

More snarling near the trailer.

"Hey!" Del shouted to anyone who would listen as he was jerked away from her and pushed in the opposite direction. "Don't anybody hurt the dogs!"

Lila glanced a few feet away and watched Brad slide into the backseat of a squad car. She hoped she would have time to tell her father so he could prepare his wife for the news. Brad had been in trouble before, so it probably wouldn't be a great shock. Or maybe it would. She had no idea what it was like to be a mother. Probably never would.

She was mesmerized by the activity. Men being frisked and cuffed—things she'd seen only on TV. Real cops and robbers probably didn't even use those words. One of the men being frisked and cuffed was her stepbrother. And dammit, one was her lover. Both were would-be thieves, and that reminded her of a song. A hymn, she thought. *And I mean to be one, too.* Saint or sinner, whatever—whoever—Del Fox was, she knew him by the love he'd shown her, and she wanted to be with him.

I'm not a thief. Believe that, no matter what.

She was dreaming. She was high on something. She'd lost her mind. How could she stand here and watch and feel completely numb? "I know that man," she muttered to herself as she watched one man lead another to a car with caged backseat. "I think that's Chet Klein."

Del whistled. She would know that sound anywhere. The shepherd was no longer snarling. Another cop opened the door to another car, and Del—with two hands tied behind his back—was allowed to direct the herder into the backseat. Proof of one of many gifts that could not be faked. Oh, he was a remarkable man.

Remarkably deceitful.

"Somebody said you're the owner."

Lila turned toward the voice. No uniform, but the tone of a cop. "I own the land. My father owns the stock."

"How about Brad Benson? He says this is his place."

"It isn't. He lives here because his mother is married to my father."

"What brought you out here tonight?"

"I knew my brother and, um, the hired hand had to be up to something."

"That would be Delano Fox?"

"Yes." She stole a glance at the cars that were being loaded up with thieves. Then she turned back to the cop. "Are you going to arrest me, too? Because if you are—"

"I would have told you."

"I have rights."

"Yes, you do. You have the right to go back home. And my partner and I have the right to go with you. We need to talk to your father."

"I was hoping I could tell him myself so he could break the news to June. Brad's mother."

"Benson is no juvenile."

"Not legally." And then, well, she couldn't help herself. "What's going to happen to Del?"

"He'll be charged with grand theft. That stock trailer is customized for rustling. There's a set of chutes that let them work the cattle right in there, alter the brands. They'd already started. Open and shut." He paused, tried to get a closer look at her. "You okay?"

"No. But I'll manage."

"I'm going to need you to ride with me. Would you like for my partner to drive your pickup?"

"It's Del's. I stole it. The keys are in it, and so is the dog. The dog goes with me."

It had been four days. Four long days filled with sadness for Lila, and for her father... Well, she hadn't been to the new house since that first night, but she could tell those days had been hell for him, too. They didn't talk about it at all. They weren't the kind to talk feelings and failures, sunken hopes and slim chances. They didn't think too much. They didn't run. They stayed put and worked. They met in Lila's kitchen and made a plan at the end of each day for what needed to be done the next. Dad wasn't going to let her sacrifice her business, and she wasn't going to let him give up his ranch. They could adjust.

It was the one good thing that had come of the incident. She had her father back. She had begun to realize that she might have seen more of him all along if she'd chosen to, instead of keeping to her own house, her own life, but she couldn't add another regret to the pile. She needed to focus on this one good thing while the days of sadness crept past. Healing took time.

Del had disappeared from her life as unexpectedly as he'd arrived, and sooner or later she would think back on the time in between. She would remember the beautiful things he'd said, sweet things he'd done, pleasure they'd shared, and the hurt would grow hazy. But she had to work through the sadness. She'd done it before, and she could do it again.

Work was a godsend. There was fence to be fixed. Between the cops and the robbers, more than a few fence posts had been upended. Returning to the scene of the crime wasn't as hard as she'd thought it would be. The sun made all the difference. That and the meadowlarks tweedling in the grass and the sweet pup that followed her everywhere.

It had been a long time since she had helped stretch wire. "How's that, Dad?" she asked on day four. "Tight enough?"

"For now," he said. Beneath the bill of his cap, his face looked tired. "Good enough for now."

"How's June?" she asked quietly as she watched her father's gloved hands release the tension on the ratcheted wire stretcher.

"I don't know. Haven't seen much of her. She

stays in the bedroom. Kinda blames me, I guess. Says I never treated Brad like a son."

"So he decided to become a cattle rustler?"

"I don't know if whether what I'm doing is right or wrong, but I know I'm not putting up bail. Like they say, been there, done that, got nothin' to show for it. His mother has resources she can tap into if she wants to." He tested the splice, playing the wire like a guitar string. "I'm guessin' it won't come cheap."

"I know it wasn't easy for you to come to that decision."

"It's time." One hand on his knee, he pushed himself up from the ground. "I ask myself, would I do anything different if he was my flesh and blood? Truth is, I would've put my foot down a long time ago. So I have to take some of the blame."

"Not now, you don't." Lila retrieved his canvas saddlebag from the fence post. "At his age, the responsibility is all his."

"What about Del?" Frank asked as he bent to gather his tools.

"I have nothing say about Del Fox. Nothing." And because he wasn't looking, she pressed her hand to her chest. "It hurts. I need to empty this out and fill it up fresh."

"I know how you feel." He loaded the wire stretcher into one canvas pouch and the big fenc-

ing pliers in the other, took the bag from her hands
and draped it over his shoulder.

She suddenly remembered that she, too, had been
carried on those shoulders.

"I don't know what's going on there," he said.
"But that Del's the real deal. And by that I mean a
good man."

"I thought so, too."

"Not perfect, mind you."

"Far from it."

"I'm not putting up bail for him, either. I'm no
fool. And I'm telling you, that man's no thief." He
waved a hand. "I know he said he'd done a little
stealing, but—"

"He said he used to be a thief, but he wasn't now.
And then he took off with Brad."

"Have you been in the shop lately?" She shook
her head. He laid his arm over her shoulders and
started waking her toward the pair of saddled horses
grazing nearby. "Come down there with me, girl.
I want to show you something he's been working
on for you."

Lila wasn't the only one who was surprised by
the pounding that sounded as though it was coming from the shop.

"Sounds like we've got company," Frank said as
he closed the corral gate. They headed for the back
door of the shop.

Del looked up from pounding support pegs into the frame of his second bookcase.

Del?

"What's going on?" Frank demanded, but he quickly tempered his tone. "They sprung ya, didn't they?"

Del smiled, but he only had eyes for Lila. "Given the chance, I like to finish what I start."

"You posted bail?" Frank asked.

"You escaped," Lila said. She could almost believe it.

Del flashed her a bright-eyed smile. "I told them they either had to give me a different job or let me go."

"Who's *them*?" Lila demanded at the same time Frank was asking, "What job?"

"I'm not a cop or a special agent, don't have a badge or a rank, but I work with people who do." He finished setting the peg and then laid the mallet aside, turning to Lila and Frank both. "I'm an ace in the law-enforcement hole. I help catch rustlers, and I'm good at it because I've been one. But that was a long time ago. I'm not a thief." He looked at Lila. "I told you that."

"My eyes deceived me, then."

"Hell, I knew there was more to it," Frank said quietly as he backed away and headed for the door. "Ha-*ha*! I knew it!"

Lila and Del stared at each other until they heard

the door close. She silently cursed the tear that escaped the corner of her eye and slid down her cheek. She wanted to throw her arms around him. She wanted to punch him in the gut.

She was shaking inside, and she hoped it didn't show. "You told me a lot of things."

"More than I should have, but I knew I could trust you." He took a step closer. "Lying is part of the job, but given who I am and what I've been, I don't have to lie too much. I really am a hired hand, and a damn good one. But that's not all." Another step. "There were things I couldn't tell you, but everything I've told you is true."

"All this, all the lovely..." Her sweeping gesture took in the bookcases, both complete and still in pieces, the dog sniffing at a pile of sawdust. "You'd have to gain people's trust, right? Your suspects, your employers, whatever we were. Was I part of the plan in this whole undercover thing? You said I wasn't sleeping with the enemy, but I don't know who—"

He grabbed her by her shoulders and kissed her, fast and full.

And then he looked into her eyes. "You know me, Lila. I'm still the man who loves you. Your father's steers are still out there eating Double F grass. Most of them still wear the Double F brand, and I'll help him fix the ones that don't. If he wants me to. If *you* want me to."

"How did you become an undercover..." She frowned. "Who do you work for anyway?"

"Have I told you it's complicated?"

"That might have been one of many words you used to get me to back off the questions."

"Well, now you can ask all twenty."

"Who do you work for anyway?"

"You know how bad livestock rustling is nowadays. It's high-tech. You saw that tricked-out stock trailer. You slide a panel inside that makes it easy to run the cattle through one at a time, slap the iron over the brand, change the markings in the blink of an eye right there on-site. Then you can truck the animals directly to a sale barn, collect one hundred percent of the value of your stolen goods.

"Down in Texas and Oklahoma they've got special rangers who handle nothing but cattle theft. Up here we've got the FBI handling cases on federal land, but they cooperate with state and local law enforcement. So they came up with a special task force. When they hire somebody like me, they can sidestep inconvenient technicalities like a felony conviction. The task force has that authority."

"So you were recruited for your particular work experience right out of prison?"

He leaned against the workbench and beckoned her with a gesture. She had to comply, right? Otherwise she wouldn't get the rest of the story.

He took her hands in his.

"I was in prison. My dad went to a relative, asked if there was anything he could do to help me out. In Indian country relatives do that, you know? But this wasn't Indian country, and this relative wasn't Indian.

"I never heard much of anything about my mother's people. I never asked. I think she took me to see them once or twice, but my memories are pretty vague when it comes to my mother. Pretty sure her family blamed my father for her death. Anyway, her father—my grandfather—he was a lawyer, a mayor somewhere, a state legislator at one time. He had connections. But he told my dad there was nothing he could do. You do the crime, you do the time. It wasn't long after that when Dad died. And then, finally, my grandfather came to see me. Said he'd had a visit with the warden, and he was real pleased to hear what a good boy I'd been since I'd gone inside. My clean jacket would help him swing the deal of a lifetime."

"Jacket?"

"Prison file. Anyway, that's what he did. He swung a deal. I was officially transferred to another prison. Nobody knew where, so my rep was secure. I was unofficially, very quietly, put on probation. I agreed to do training and five years' service. I paid restitution, and after five years my record was expunged. And that never happens with a felony conviction."

"You said you've been out almost seven years."

"It's not a bad job." He squeezed her hands. "Until you have to steal from your girl's father and arrange for her brother's arrest."

"*Step*brother. He's been in so much trouble, and my father keeps bailing him out. But not this time. I really hope he learns his lesson this time."

"It's a hard way to learn."

"But you did. And you made up for your mistakes. By expunged, you mean erased?"

"It means it's not public. It's sealed, but it'll always be there." He drew a deep breath. "I don't pack a gun, but I do carry baggage. I didn't want to bring it into your house. I didn't mean to touch you with it. But I have, and I'm sorry."

"It was awful seeing you in handcuffs." Another tear slipped past her eyelid, and she could do nothing about it. Her hands were tied.

"You thought I got caught stealing cattle. I belonged in handcuffs."

"It was unreal, like a bad dream. I've watched you work with your hands, handle a horse, play with Asap. I've felt them—" she lifted his hand and tucked it against her chest "—touch me all over. It was the handcuffs that tore me up inside. Seeing you like that."

"I don't know how many times I've been arrested, and even though I know it's just part of the job now, I still haven't gotten used to it. You weren't mad at me?"

"That came later. I remembered some basic math facts. Put two and two together and realized feelings don't change the facts. And now I know that you came here to do a tricky job, and you used me."

"How?"

"To get information? I don't know. I'm the boss's daughter."

"Who was barely speaking to the rest of the family." He sighed and rolled his eyes. "Okay, you're right. I have to get in good with people so I can figure out what's going on and who might be involved. That's the way I operate. So maybe at first… Aw, hell, Lila, I liked you right off, and it wasn't all about your pretty face or your high-headed sass. You got into my head that first day, and after that I had to keep reminding myself why I was here."

"Why are you here now?"

"I want to finish these bookcases. Come here." He drew her by the hand over to the nearly finished bookcase he'd been working on earlier. "You can adjust the shelves for different size books. I can paint them any color you want or do a wood finish, bolt them to the wall so they can't topple over. I cut the pieces for two more, and they'll all fit together in that space you said…" He trailed off and took her shoulders in his hands. "You wanted me to stay. Now I can. Do you still want me to?"

"My father needs help, and he'd like nothing better than for you to stay on. But you're not really a ranch hand, so I can't see you—"

"Then you're not looking. I've fulfilled my commitment, but I need a reason to refuse the next assignment. And I never know when another one will come along. Maybe it's time I changed jobs." He raised his eyebrows. "What do you think? Maybe I could be an actor. Or a dog trainer. Or maybe just a damn good ranch hand."

He slid his arms around her shoulders and smiled. "Funny. Frank says *you* would like it if I stayed around. You say *he* wants me to stay on. After everything that's gone down, I need to know who wants what from me. What do *you* want, Lila?"

She slipped her arms around his waist. "I want colors. I've already picked them out from a brochure."

"From the Swedish furniture company?"

She laughed. "I still haven't figured out that dresser."

"We could do it together."

"We could do many things together."

"I need an answer, Lila. I have other questions for you, but first things first." He kissed her damp cheek. "I know you love me. Will you dare to trust me?"

"I want you to stay. Next question."

"I'm going to help your father and fix what needs

fixing, build what needs building and marry the woman I love whenever she decides she'll have me." He glanced at Asap. "And my dog. He's part of the package."

"So what's the question?"

"No more questions," he whispered, and their kiss became the answer.

* * * * *

MILLS & BOON®

Want to get more from Mills & Boon?

Here's what's available to you if you join the exclusive **Mills & Boon eBook Club** today:

✦ *Convenience – choose your books each month*
✦ *Exclusive – receive your books a month before anywhere else*
✦ *Flexibility – change your subscription at any time*
✦ *Variety – gain access to eBook-only series*
✦ *Value – subscriptions from just £1.99 a month*

So visit **www.millsandboon.co.uk/esubs** today to be a part of this exclusive eBook Club!

MILLS & BOON®

Need more New Year reading?

We've got just the thing for you!
We're giving you 10% off your next eBook or
paperback book purchase on the Mills & Boon
website. So hurry, visit the website today and type
SAVE10 in at the checkout for your exclusive

10% DISCOUNT

www.millsandboon.co.uk/save10

Ts and Cs: Offer expires 31st March 2015.
This discount cannot be used on bundles or sale items.

MILLS & BOON®

Cherish™

EXPERIENCE THE ULTIMATE RUSH OF FALLING IN LOVE

A sneak peek at next month's titles...

In stores from 16th January 2015:

- **Best Friend to Wife and Mother?** – Caroline Anderson
  and **Marry Me, Mackenzie!** – Joanna Sims

- **Her Brooding Italian Boss** – Susan Meier
  and **Fortune's Little Heartbreaker** – Cindy Kirk

In stores from 6th February 2015:

- **The Daddy Wish** – Brenda Harlen
  and **The Heiress's Secret Baby** – Jessica Gilmore

- **A Pregnancy, a Party & a Proposal** – Teresa Carpenter
  and **The Fireman's Ready-Made Family** – Jules Bennett

0115/23